Poor Angels and other stories

Poor Angels

and other stories

Chris Dolan

Polygon
EDINBURGH

Published by Polygon
22 George Square
Edinburgh

Set in Meridien by WestKey Ltd, Falmouth, Cornwall
Printed and bound in Great Britain by Short Run Press, Exeter

A CIP record for this title is available

The Publisher acknowledges subsidy from the

towards the publication of this book.

Contents

Poor Angels

1

SOUTHSIDE 11.55. A flank of semis keeps watch over the night, cushion and lace fortresses standing shoulder to shoulder. Not a sound, save the viola darkness and a smir of rain like a mother's hush.

A gate swings back on its hinges. The semi behind it opens a sleepy curtain eyelid, pouring honey light out from an upstairs window. A woman, babe in arms, looks out. Seeing nothing but the breeze, she bows her head to look down into the sea-green garden and the sweet protective face of an angel, who stretches his wings protectively up towards mother and child. The woman smiles and with the fall of the curtain, darkness returns.

NORTHSIDE 12.00 Midnight. Another street. Could be another planet. The smir here an aching drizzle. Not a soul in sight. Only one building remains standing, the glum light of its GENTLEMEN sign overpowered by the stench: the excreta of diseased bowels and collapsed kidneys, wine vomits and the spillage of old men's fumblings.

A figure, hooded and draped, slowly materialises out of the black. He holds something in his arms, cradles it like a child, as he runs down the steps to the door of the sunken toilet.

3

The sudden, desperate scream of a human infant.

4

Gordon leapt out of bed and was at Sammy's side a fraction before Cathy. He stumbled to a cassette player on a bedside table next to the cot. He pressed 'play' and let out the slush and slither of womb music. Cathy's own womb music, recorded by one of Gordon's mates who doubles as a boom operator when he can't get a hire as a producer. The room filled with a soft, blue watery sound, like a distant cistern, miraculously working on Sammy. The child's eyes lolled in his head as his eyelids came down, but as he drifted back into sleep, the tape snarled up like a bad attack of cramps. Cathy automatically hugged her belly, and Sammy screamed louder than ever.

– I'll take him downstairs. Cathy bent over the cot to lift him.

– Hang on.

Gordon closed his eyes, held his hand up in the air and thought hard. Then he made a low-pitched bubbling sound in the back of his throat, gargling the phlegm that had gathered during the night, dubbing onto Sammy's mind the missing womb soundtrack. It began to work: Sammy looked up at him, interested. Gordon, getting confident, added a low hum to his splutters. Sammy's wails trailed off.

– Sing. Gordon whispered.

– What?

– Sing!

Cathy joined in sheepishly, making a WHOOSHing noise through her teeth, to accompany her husband's gurgling. Sammy turned to look, intrigued, at her. Pleased, Cathy added a rhythmic WHEESH to the WHOOSHES. Sammy laughed. Cathy wanted to too, but Gordon was being dead serious. If this was what it took for an extra hour's sleep then to buggery with pride. He kept going, but Cathy couldn't keep it up and doubled over with silent laughter. The game was up, Sammy was wide awake and having fun. Gordon stopped gargling and had an attack of coughing instead. Sammy clapped, delighted.

– Fuck it.

Gordon got up and went to the window, opened the curtains. It was bright outside already. Cathy lifted Sammy and returned to the bed, still whooshing.

– My angel! Gordon said, without turning from the window.

– Yes, dear?

– Not you. The angel. It's gone.

– What do you mean, gone? It was there last night. It couldn't just have flown away.

Gordon turned and ran to the bedroom door, belted down the stairs. Cathy heard the front door being flung open, got up and took Sammy over to the window. True enough, instead of the stone angel that usually stood in the middle of the garden, there was only Gordon, in his pyjamas, his hair sculpted into a study of bewilderment by sleep and night-sweat. He put his hands up into the air, then let them fall heavily, shaking his head ferociously from side to side. An elaborate mime designed to alert the world, or Cathy at least, that life these days was coming to a pretty shitty pass. He looked up and his and Cathy's eyes met. His furious; hers a little scared.

Half an hour later, they were sitting over a breakfast prepared for the sake of form, left untouched even by Sammy. Cathy and Gordon watched him in silence as he played thoughtfully with his apple-and-cereal Milupa, like at any minute he might come up with the explanation.

– Seventeen thousand pesetas that thing cost me.

– Probably the local lads playing a joke. Cathy tried to sound easy-osy. – They'll have ditched it in another garden.

– And that's not counting the excess baggage. If I'd known how much that was, I'd never have bought you it.

– So you've said.

– Well.

The poncy angel had been a thorn in his flesh since Cathy'd seen it in Fuengirola. He'd rather have walked through the airport with a sombrero and a BÉSAME MUCHO T-shirt on, than carry a stone bloody angel through a bunch of hard-faced Glaswegians, tanked up for the journey home. And that was just the beginning. He had to put up with every prat within a four-block radius slagging his taste in garden furniture. Then there were the visitors – he arranged all their dinner parties to start after the hours of darkness, even in summer, so they wouldn't see the fucker on their way in. Now some tadger comes along and steals the bastard. Jesus!

At the front door, Gordon picked up his briefcase and put on his jacket, Cathy beside him with Sammy, trying to act as if it were a normal morning. They didn't notice the hooded figure through the glass door behind them, making its way up the path. They nearly jumped out their skins when it rang the bell. Sammy took to screaming blue-murder again. Gordon tried to open the door angrily – like, slam it open.

– What!

The postman, uniform under his anorak, took a step backwards.

– Package for Mrs. Magee.

Gordon grabbed it. The postman scuttled off. Cathy shook her head at Gordon, as he examined the parcel. Heinz babyfood stickers. He gave it to Cathy, and stepped outside. Cathy said

– Not got a kiss for Sammy-wammy?

Gordon pulled a thin smile on over his temper, and leaned in to kiss the child. But Sammy wasn't in the mood, and screamed louder in his father's face. Gordon about-turned and marched off, mumbling

– Wee shite.

5

Down the stairs, the door of the public convenience was locked and bolted behind an old rusted padlocked shutter. Between the door and the shutter, months of refuse – beer cans, condoms, paper – lay undisturbed by wind or rain in the sunken doorway. A passerby – had there been any in this deserted corner of town – would have assumed the convenience was simply no longer convenient.

The passerby would have been wrong. The City Fathers closed down the infamous Neal Street cottage nigh on two years ago – an inspired coup that had done more to frustrate the casual vice scene in Glasgow's Northside than all the expensive beat work of the previous decade. Once the decision had been taken, a particularly straight-talking Councillor made a press call, inviting the local media to witness the final locking-up ceremony, proclaiming it a decisive blow to every shirtlifter, crackhead, pimp and weirdo in the city. Neal Street Cottage's days as the Mecca of part-time pushers and rendezvous for men with more than conversation in mind were over.

On the road behind it, a grey second hand Saab trundled by. Gordon, tucked up inside, let his anger subside under the lull of the 2-litre engine. He was glad the stupid statue was gone. He'd tell everybody he'd elbowed it, like he always said he would. Turning the corner, he didn't notice the light on inside the toilet. If he had looked closely in through the filthy windows he might have seen the hooded figures passing bundles down along the row of leaking urinals.

6

Sammy tried to help with the opening of the parcel. The child's uncanny. Surely he doesn't actually recognise Heinz baby-food stickers? Nah. It's the crinkle and crunch of sellotape and paper. A lot of layers of the stuff. What have they put in here for God's sake? One wee can of creamed Turkey and Vegetable, and packed it up to look like a month's supply? Yoghurt-pot Capitalism, as Gordon likes to say. The system's got a false arse and they think nobody notices.

The last layer of paper was red and sticky. Cathy thought a jar of bolognese must have broken. But inside, a gouged-out eye of a stone statue stared up at her out of the red gunge. Red threads had been attached to it, like severed arteries.

She wanted to scream, but couldn't. There was no air in her lungs. She grabbed Sammy – more for her benefit than his – knocking the eye off the table, the bloody gunge splatting the floor. Then she saw the card. Nicely typed up, and protected from the red mess by a neat little plastic holder that you get on library cards and bus passes. The print was small, but perfectly legible, even lying on the floor at her feet.

FOLLOW INSTRUCTIONS, OR THE ANGEL GETS IT

7

– It's your wife.

Leanne had the knack of making 'wife' sound like 'mother'.

– She sounds a wee bitty upset.

He *knew* this statue thing would get to her. He considered for a moment, as he took the phone, telling Cathy never to call him at work. But that would have been too naff. They were on the eternal look-out for a reason to get at him, Eraserhead and Leanne and Sally and the rest of them. Cathy, too, for all he knew. Even Sammy hated him today.

Never stopped any of them taking the Magee Shilling, but. He hired them, and they came running, no matter what the project. This one was the worst. Duck-necked lavatory cleaner for fuck's sake. There was no argument that the last thing the world needed to know about now was duck-necked lavatory cleaner. To get into those difficult corners. At least he was earning a living. Eraserhead and the rest of them were forever working on development money for some half-cocked screenplay that would never happen. They couldn't survive without him. But they thought he was a traitor. Walked away from a promising film career to make funny money in advertising.

And now this.

– A ransom note? For the angel?

He had the mouthpiece all but inside his mouth, for privacy. But he could feel Eraserhead behind his back, his Bob Monkhouse sincere-worried face, Leanne's eyes frosting over with submerged laughter.

– Christ, no! He whispered. – Get a grip, Cath. What will I tell them? Excuse me, Officer, but I'd like to report a kidnapped angel?

He laughed with Eraserhead and Leanne when he put the phone down.

– Great crack, eh? Have to admit, wish I'd thought of it myself. There's a few up my way who could do with being brought down a peg or two.

– Tough at the top, said Eraserhead

He went out the back to his car. Eraserhead was always coming out with that tough-at-the-top crap when Leanne was around. Meaning: 'I'm shagging her, and you're not.' Meaning: 'You've got spondulicks but no cred'. Eraserhead had better watch his step – he wasn't *that* good an editor. Gordon had christened Brian Eraserhead to indicate that he wasn't just a movie anorak, but an ugly bastard into the bargain. But Brian saw the potential in it. He told everybody to call him Eraserhead – little middle-class wannabe's like Leanne get a kick out of shagging an Eraserhead.

His car phone was ringing when he opened the door.

– Gordon Magee? It was a cultured voice. – We've a friend of yours here.

– Excuse me?

– Maybe you'd better come and take him home.

Someone's gone and poked his eye out. Poor little angel.

– Now hang on, you.

– Tell your wife and little Sammy not to worry. Daddy will bring their angel home safe and sound. Just look for the sign.

8

Inside Neal Street cottage, the man with the pony-tail, loose black suit and buttoned-up shirt, clicked the mobile phone off and called the staff to attention.

– Right. Let's get moving.

There were about eight or nine of them, all, like the man, under thirty-five, sitting around on sinks and leaning against the walls. They put down their mugs of tea, got up, put on their parkas, pulled their hoods up, and began organising themselves.

Each of them took up their positions in front of urinals, or inside cubicles. One of them stood beside the exit, passing in bundles wrapped in blankets from a colleague outside. Everyone worked quietly and efficiently, passing the bundles down the line at a smooth, regular pace. They enjoyed their work, stopping every now and then to share a laugh.

– We'll get the show on the road, then, will we? said the man in the suit, and entered the cubicle marked DISABLED.

9

Cathy wished she had waited a bit before phoning Gordon. He'd cast that call up to her for months now. Sure, she had a bout of the screaming ab-dabs every now and then. Everyone needed a safety valve. Gordon disappeared on overnight drunks from time to time to get rid of his demons. She had the odd flakey every now and then to get rid of hers. But Gordon had her down as a neurotic mess.

Like the angel thing. She just liked it. Thought it would look nice in the garden. Homely. But Gordon kept inferring that she had some deep-seated need for divine protection. Gordon hated anything that was even vaguely religious. The world is as it is. That was Gordon's position. That's the position all of them take. That prat Eraserhead, and Deek – what a laugh Gordon and Deek had at her expense over her wanting her womb music recorded. For heaven's sake, she'd just read in a magazine that it would help the baby sleep once it was born. And a good investment it turned out to be.

Still, she shouldn't have made the call while she was still upset. Now Gordon'll just outdo her on the upset stakes. She was alright now. She could see the funny side. When she got the little devils who dreamed it up, she'd take the face off them. But kids will be kids, eh? Some day in the future she'd have to clean up some silly scam that Sammy had got himself into. She looked out the window. Everybody else had one of those stupid stone lions on the gateposts stolen at one time or another. But they had to go and take their angel.

10

Gordon was driving carefully. Cathy'd be climbing the walls but the last thing he needed was another speeding ticket and getting struck off or whatever it is they do to offending drivers. The bastards, they'd got him rattled. All they had to do was mention Sammy's name.

He drove past the deserted toilet. He could put on a bit of speed here. The area was like a ghost town, not even the cops came down this way. He leant over and opened the glove compartment, fumbled around for his cigars. He didn't smoke any more. Didn't even miss it much now. All he missed was the little ritual of opening up that lovely, neat little cardboard box, pulling out the little white cylinders, and flicking his gold lighter into flame. He got some of that thrill by taking the odd cigar. Not lighting it, just opening the box and fingering the smooth, slim panatella, peeling off its little cover, putting it in his mouth.

He was coming back into town now. He was maybe travelling a bit too fast, manoeuvring around the cars, lane hopping a bit. He was vaguely aware that the cigar felt different in his hand. Heavier. He still wasn't used to the feel of cigars. He put it in his mouth, but it felt too cold, hard.

– JEESWEPT!

He had to swerve to stop himself going into the back of a car in front. The cigar was a finger. Grey-blue, hard and cold, like it belonged to a stiff. He threw it down and it landed with a bump on his accelerator foot. He weaved amongst the cars with his left hand, all of them blasting their horns at him. He managed to pull over, open the door and kick the finger into the gutter. He closed his eyes for a moment to get over the shakes. When he opened them, the car he had almost run into the back of had pulled in right in front of him. Guy was probably going to come and start shouting the odds. But no-one came. The passenger in the back seat was looking round at him. Then the car started to move slowly away, and he realised the passenger wasn't a person. His angel was propped up in the back, staring out at him with one eye, its hand held up in a wave. One of its fingers missing.

– Bastards!

He crashed the gears into first, and took off after the car.

– God, what on earth is all this supposed to *mean*?

Leanne leant over and switched the visuals on the Avid editing machine to full screen.

– It's not supposed to *mean* anything.

– I know, but seriously. A street full of people walking about with toilet pans on their heads doesn't suggest *cleanliness* to me.

– The bowls are clean enough to put your head into?

– You'd know all about that.

– Thank*you*.

Eraserhead switched the machine back over to the timeline.

– The visuals are just supposed to grab your attention. That's all. You sell the product *underneath* the images. It's the clinch that matters. You just make it look like it's the images that matter.

– You're as full of pish as he is.

– Where did you get these?

The man in the suit took a thick bundle of disorderly files with a Dead Kennedys sticker on the back from one of the hooded workers.

– Electrical engineering notes. Only up to first year, like, when I jacked it.

– They'll do nicely.

– I thought Jakesy could do the missus. He looks the part.

– Not Jakesy. Ka.

The hood smiled and called out

– Ka! That's you Jakesy, ya cunt.

The rest of the workers, who were drinking out of cans and plastic cups in the wash area, laughed. One of them, with a large scar on his face, approached the man in the suit. The man in the suit looked impressed.

– Tell him where you got your facial, Ka. Said the hood.

– Slashed. Ka growled at the man in the suit, like he might be to blame.

The hood egged him on.

– Go on.

Ka looked down and shuffled a bit.

– By a hairdresser.

The man in the suit smiled

– She was a trainee.

– She was a fucking maddo!

The man in the suit patted him on the shoulder.

– Well, it'll come in handy today. Remember what you've got to do?

– No problemo, Eric.

– Khan. Remember? Shere Khan.

– Oh aye.

Ka pulled his hood up and made for the exit. Shere Khan turned and went into the DISABLED loo.

13

The Ford Mondeo was giving him the run around. He'd been up by what was left of Springburn, twice round the Red Road flats, back down through Pollock and over the river to Shawlands and Battlefield. Now they were taking him down Castlehill Avenue, right past his own house.

– Fucking hilarious boys.

He slowed down as much as he could without losing the Mondeo, and blasted his horn at the house. Every other nosy bugger in the street came to their windows. But no Cathy. He'd already phoned her, about an hour ago, not long after he'd started the chase. Spun her a line about passing by the police station, which was why he'd be later back than expected. He was hardly going to tell her what was *actually* happening. She'd go doo-lally. He'd suggested she go to her Mum's – where she always went when she got into one of her fankles – which she must have done.

Now the Mondeo was heading back to his office again.

– Yeh, yeh. Round the houses, up the garden path, then back round in a circle. Arseholes.

Actually, there was only one arsehole, not counting the angel. At a corner in town he caught a glimpse of the driver's face as he went round. Wee weedy guy. Surprised he was old enough to have a licence. Probably didn't.

It was nearly dark now. How long had he been driving for? He checked the dashboard clock. Half four. Jesus. No, half three. He'd never got round to putting the clock back last month. Christ, though. Dark for half three.

14

Sammy had had enough sludge. He had an effective way of letting you know – he spat the last mouthful out at you. Boy's not silly. He finds ingenious ways of communicating. She threw the remains of his plate into the bin, over the mutilated eye which winked back up at her through the dregs and slops. She threw the plate in over it.

It was already pitch outside. She'd told Gordon she'd no intention of going to her Mum's, but maybe she would after all. Pass by the police station on the way, see if Gordon was still there. Maybe they were keeping him in for questioning. God, she hadn't thought of that. What if it *was* Gordon? He hated that angel. Don't be silly, she just had a downer on him today. She got her coat, and Sammy's things together. He was smelly, but she'd wait till she got to her Mum's before she changed him. He'd just eaten, so there was probably more to come. Just have to put up with the smell in the car.

She felt better once she was out. Driving was the one activity that kept Sammy quiet. She could concentrate on the road and keep her mind off other things. The traffic was heavy. It wasn't four yet, but these days, what with flexi-time and everything, the rush hour went on all afternoon. She remembered something Martha told her. Martha had taken a voluntary job on some telephone helpline or other. The Guilt Line she called it. All these middle-aged men phoning in to confess. Martha said, you'd be amazed, ninety per cent of males in this city don't come straight home from work. They stop off at toilets and parks to, you know . . .

– No. What?

– You *know* . . . Play with each other.

No. She didn't know. It shocked her at the time, but now it struck her as hilarious, all these accountants and lawyers standing around in parks and loos with their hands in each others' flies like some weird masonic handshake. There's no doubt – it's a strange world out there. That's why she liked the angel. A kind of protection from it all. Gordon was right though – it didn't do any good. The weirdos went and kidnapped it.

The traffic thinned out at Bearsden. She turned right, up into her parents' street – a never-ending terrace of newish pebble-dashed little houses. The road was empty of any other moving vehicles. So she could see the bundle clearly where it lay in the middle of the street. She slowed. God, it looked like a baby, wrapped up. She didn't want to stop, but it was smack bang in the middle of the road. She stopped the car short of it. Checked Sammy – he was gurgling happily in the back. She got out, and approached the bundle.

Behind her, a hooded figure crept out of the bushes in front of one of the houses, tip-toed silently to the car. He got in the driver's seat that Cathy had left open, and slid easily over the top of her seat onto the floor at the back, beneath Sammy.

Sammy was about to scream, when Ka showed him his nice shiny chib. He let Sammy touch it, which kept him quiet.

Cathy gingerly kicked the bundle aside. The contents spilled out over the kerb and pavement: a stone lion like one of those in her street, hacked to pieces.

– OH MOTHER OF GOD

She ran back to the car, jumped in, slammed the door shut and shot off up the street. Trembling, she checked the rear-view mirror. Sammy was looking down at the car floor and laughing happily. Then she saw what Sammy was laughing at. Some kind of metal pole, sticking up behind her seat. She started to look round, when Ka popped up and smiled at her. He grabbed her round the chin and mouth.

– Don't frighten the baby.

15

Gordon sat in his car at one side of the Neal Street Public Convenience, keeping an eye on the rear end of the Mondeo which he could see sticking out from behind the other side. Both engines were still running. They had been sitting like this for nearly quarter of an hour. The dashboard clock said 9.30, meaning 8.30. He didn't know what else he could do but wait. Sure as fate, the minute he opened the car door to make a run at it, the Mondeo would speed off. He considered phoning Cath at her Mum's, but thought better of it. When it came to the heebie-jeebies, Cath was a mere novice compared to her mother. Better wait and see how things panned out here. If the Mondeo took off again, he wasn't going to follow it. They'd had their fun. He'd just wait a bit longer to see why it had stopped here.

There seemed to be a light on inside the john. That's just the sort of botch-up the Council would make: close down a public convenience to save money, then leave the fucking light burning for two years. He passed this place every morning and every night, and never gave it a thought. Now, though, he wondered if this was the place he and Deek and a few others ended up in that night. Years ago. They'd been on the pish, and were waiting for a taxi to go back to Deek's place, when this bus came by. None of them had been on a bus for yonks, and had no idea where they went to these days. But, rat-arsed, they jumped on it, then back off ten minutes later when Gordon was dying for a slash. They'd laughed themselves silly at being stuck in no-man's land, falling about, scared shitless. Then this brasser happened by. What a sight she was: tits hanging out, skirt above her huge arse, ripped tights. He remembered that – tights, not even nylons. Tights with the bum ripped out them. She asked them if they were looking for business, and they slagged her rotten. Then, someone, Deek or Malcolm, staked a 10-spot dare for anyone to give her a feel. She was the ugliest bitch Gordon had ever seen, but she kind of turned him on. He was steaming, for chrissakes. Anyway, they had a bit of fun with her. Nothing serious, mind. And she took it in good heart. God knows how much money she made out of them, they were all slinging brownbacks at her, when a taxi finally came by and picked them up. He'd been that drunk, he couldn't remember the next morning where it had all happened. It could have been here. There was a closed-up toilet, because he had to piss up against the wall. The whole place had looked like a shit-house. Like here. Then again, half the city looks like this.

He dialled the office number to see if Eraserhead and Leanne were still there. Probably having it off over the Steinbeck. But before the tone came, he saw the wee guy from the Mondeo making a dash to the toilet, carrying the angel under his arm. He let the phone drop and raced after him.

– COME BACK HERE, YA WEE SHITE!

16

Leanne put the phone back down.

– Somebody shouting 'ya wee shite'.

Eraserhead lifted it back up, and listened.

– Kids.

He put the phone back down, and put his arm round Leanne's waist. She wriggled away.

– Leave it out, Brian.

When women reverted to calling him by his real name, it meant the game was up. Nobody loves a Brian. This was not a good day.

17

Ka had made Cathy drive back from Bearsden via Summerston, Maryhill and George's Cross. Past Daydream Productions, Gordon's office, where she caught a glimpse of Eraserhead at the window guzzling Scotch straight from the bottle. Then along the Expressway to this half-demolished part of town she hated. Her heart sank when Ka instructed her to pull up here. He led her down the steps of the old toilets to the entrance marked LADIES. Absurdly, she half-hoped he'd wait outside.

She'd been on a knife-edge when she was driving, but now that she was inside the LADIES, she felt kind of calm. She told herself that she really ought to panic. Any decent mother would go bananas being kept hostage in a public convenience by a loony with a twelve-inch crowbar six inches from her baby's head.

But the place was quite warm. It was full of horrible dripping sounds, but apart from that, it wasn't as bad as she'd expected. She'd heard Gordon's Dad say that working down the sewers wasn't as terrible you'd think. Once you're in the shit, you don't notice the smell. Sammy seemed quite happy. Ka – or whatever it was he called himself – let her go and get the changing bag from the car. Went with her, of course. On the way back he asked her to wait outside the door of the GENTLEMEN's, which was gracious of him. She could hear him talking to someone inside. When he came back out, he said they had to move her car out of view. He told her to drive a few streets away, without lights, Sammy calm on his knee. She strained to see the clock on the blacked-out dashboard. No chance. Pitch.

Back inside the LADIES, Ka was quite nice, really. He handed her the nappy, got rid of the soiled one, opened the jar of Sudocrem for her. Sammy had quite taken to him, not at all put off by the nasty-looking scar on his face. She wanted to ask how he got it, but thought that would be too much like fraternising.

She was here. She didn't know why. This is the real world. All you can do is sit it out and see what happens.

The light was on in the GENTLEMEN's when Gordon flew down the steps after the hood. But everything went suddenly black when he reached the door. He took a step inside. He couldn't see a thing, and the place was deathly quiet except for dripping noises. Then, as he turned to get the hell out of there, a grinding roar echoed around the chamber. He watched as the iron shutter was dragged closed. He ran to it and shook it desperately, but it didn't budge.

He stood, shivering, putting his hands to his head, expecting a blow at any moment. Nothing. He listened, but there was no sound.

– Hullo?

A woman's voice:

– Bear with us a moment, Gordon. We seem to have a black out.

– Who said that?

The lights came back on. Gordon stood stunned – the place was full of people. A woman, presumably the one who had spoken a moment ago, was standing next to him. She gently took his arm and led him up through the toilet. Gordon followed, staring incredulously at the hooded factory line work industriously away at their urinal stations, popping in and out of cubicles with parcels, files, messages on Post-it pads. The whole scene made him feel sleepy, dreamy. The woman stopped and knocked on the door of the DISABLED cubicle. The flush sounded. She waited until the final gurgle and splurts died away before opening the door and standing back to let Gordon enter first.

Shere Khan sat on the toilet bowl behind a grey workstation, tapping on a laptop. He looked up and smiled.

– Mr Magee.

He closed the lid of the laptop, picked up the open folder

lying next to it, lifted the lid of the cistern behind him, and carefully filed the folder away.

– Good of you to come and collect your property yourself. There's a five per cent discount for self-collection.

Gordon felt himself coming round, like waking up the morning after a night on the batter.

– Discount?

Khan turned to the woman.

– Village Girl, bring Mr. Magee's property immediately. Castlehill Section. Mr. Bagheera will give you the precise stock number.

Village Girl nodded and went off.

– I'm afraid we've given you a bit of a runaround today, Gordon. You don't mind if I call you Gordon? I hate to stand on ceremony. So, what shall we say – five hundred pounds seem fair to you? That's including the 5 per cent discount. We accept most major credit cards and cheques accompanied by a current cheque card.

– What for?

– The safe return of your angel, of course.

– You must be joking, the fucking thing only cost about eighty quid.

Khan sat back down behind his desk with a weary sigh. He opened a drawer and took out a pack of cigarettes, offered one to Gordon, who took it, shakily.

– We're running a business here, Gordon. An unlikely setting I agree, but we do know our market. The 3 P's: Place, Product, Price. Geographically, we're on a winner. Your street – Castlehill Avenue – alone has been very good to us. Roaring trade. The Product, I think you'll agree, is effective. We seldom have our clients getting back in touch to complain. As for Price, well, this is a low-risk, high-turnover market. Five hundred pounds for the service we've delivered to you – all our research shows that's the least the market will bear.

– Then do your research again. You won't get a tuppenny fuck out of me.

– I note a certain lack of conviction in your voice, Gordon. However, anticipating a fighting spirit from a successful movie director like yourself, we took out a little insurance policy.

Khan nodded towards Village Girl, who left the cubicle, immediately replaced by another hood. This one a man. Khan slid the heavy lid off the cistern behind him and pulled out a fat, disorganised file. Gordon saw some kind of label was stuck to the back of it – something about Dead Kennedys.

– There are a lot of details recorded in this folder that Mrs Magee doesn't know about you. A lot of things you don't know about yourself. Some of them verifiable, others less so. Don't get me wrong, Gordon, I'm not saying you're a bad man with lots of things to hide. Just an average man, with average things to hide.

The cubicle door opened and Village girl led in Cathy and Sammy. The ferocious somersault inside Gordon's chest translated itself outwardly into his cigarette dropping from his lips. The hood bent down and picked it back up off the sodden floor, flicking off the excess yellow moisture from the tip before re-inserting it into Gordon's mouth.

Khan came round from behind his desk.

– Well, I think this little boy needs his beddy-byes. Just a few last instructions. We would like to draw our fee from your joint account. Countersigned by both of you. Village Girl has been good enough to get your chequebook from your car for you, Gordon. Naturally, you will consider cancelling the cheque in the morning. But you won't, because we could all do without the hassle of going through the same old process all over again. And next time, the price will be much higher. Secondly, I would be obliged if you would place the angel, unrepaired, in its old place in the garden. A sign, as it were. Like blood on your door, that you are one of us now.

Village Girl handed Gordon his cheque book. Khan handed him a pen. Gordon took it, and poked him with it. It was a feeble action that provoked a general shuffle of embarrassment. Cathy took the pen from him.

– Just sign the cheque, Gordon.

She handed the pen back and Gordon signed. The hood picked up the angel and put it into Gordon's arms, then moved back from the door, to let them pass.

– Perhaps just one last teeny favour? Khan spoke again.

– I believe you're working on a film at present for Duncan's Cleaning Products? You couldn't possibly negotiate a cheap deal on our behalf for their duck-necked range could you? As you can see our premises aren't as spick and span as we'd like. We'd bulk buy, of course.

19

The bar was closing. Sally put her coat on and made for the door. Leanne downed her vodka in one and joined her.

– So how come you eventually gave Eraserhead the heave today?

– Just one of those days. Somebody had to suffer.

It was a dirty wet night outside. They made their way to the corner, where a hooded figure stood in the shadow of a close door.

– I thought it was Gordon you were after anyway?

– No chance, though. Him and Cathy are like that. Happy fucking families.

Leanne stood back while Sally went up and did business with the hooded man.

– Come on back to my place. Blow them all away.

When they arrived back at the house, Cathy took Sammy out of his baby seat in the Micra, and Gordon lifted the angel out of the boot of the Saab.

    – What a nightmare. Gordon said. – Were they *real*?

    – What else could they be?

    Cathy walked up towards the house. Gordon took the angel towards the garden. He called to her

    – Should I phone the police then?

    – No.

    – No.

21

NORTHSIDE 11.55 The Neal Street cottage light glows dimly, illuminating tiny drops of rain in the night air, so that they flash and dance around in the quiet, empty streets. And then the light goes out and the growing laughter from within the cottage echoes merrily around the demolished wasteland.

22

SOUTHSIDE. MIDNIGHT. It is cold outside in the sea-green garden, where Gordon is on his knees, balancing the angel precariously back on its pedestal. He looks out into the street. Lions on the gate-posts with their ears severed, broken children's swings, flower-beds half-dug up, cracked window-panes. The most desirable street in the district, and look at it, it's in tatters.

    A light comes on upstairs. Cath appears at the window, Sammy asleep in her arms, and looks down at Gordon crouching in the wet grass. Their eyes meet for a moment. Then she turns away, and closes the curtains, plunging Gordon and his angel into darkness. He glances up at the angel. The rain is gathering in its empty eye socket, trickling down its cheek.

Sleet and Snow

She sat on the bed and he knelt in front of her. He took her left foot in his hands, which were big enough to go right round her from ankle to toe, and he pulled like billy-o. The boots weren't that tight, but his arms ached. He had no strength left in his grip. It always took him by surprise, this powerlessness. His arms didn't *feel* weak on a day-to-day basis. Only when he had to pull at something – like the heavy saucepan from the bottom of the cupboard, or the toilet door when the carpet rode up and stuck it – then they felt like they were half-empty. Like his veins were too big for the dregs of blood that sloshed around inside them.

    – What's with the tight shoes anyway, Missus? Trying to make your feet look thin?

    – I've squeezed and squashed every bit of myself half me life. Why stop wi' me feet?

He used to like that – seeing all that soft flesh crammed into hard, tight clothes, like a spongy cushion stuffed into a leather cover. Breasts siphoned into boned bras, buttocks jacked up into ribbed pants, stomach squeezed into girdles. Then looking forward to it all springing back into life again at the end of the day. Now her getting dressed served the opposite purpose – to make it look as if there was some flesh left beneath the clothes. That, and to cover up the pain. She had more pain than flesh now.

Their lives had become very physical in their old age. All this helping each other on and off with shoes and jerseys, rubbing on ointments, clutching each other on stairs:

– Can't seem to keep our hands off each other these days, Missus.

They both wore the same kinds of clothes, now. Slip-on jerseys and trousers with elastic waists that didn't require the use of strong fingers. She'd laugh and tell him:

– No point in you getting kinky all of a sudden and trying on all my clothes. We're unisex now.

She pulled off the whole geriatric show much better than he could. A dab of lipstick, a water-colour rinse, taking the supporting arm like it was a lady's prerogative and not the result of aching bones. All her life she had been the independent one, doing her own thing whenever it came up her hump. Now she was the lady who expected to be waited upon.

She'd got into his taxi one day outside Central Station wearing a skirt and cardigan and slippers when the snow was piled six inches high.

– Where to?

– Eh, Dennistoun. I think.

– Couldn't be a bit more specific, could you?

– Dumbarton Road.

– Dumbarton Road's not in Dennistoun.

– Is there a Dennistoun Road in Dumbarton, then?

– Came out for your ciggies and forgot where you live, did you?

She looked at him for a minute, then threw her head back laughing.

– And I don't even smoke.

She was English. Chubbier, taller than most women he knew; her hair different. Not blonde, not brunette. Honey, she would tell him later. Honey in some lights, strawberry blonde in others. This was just after the war when you couldn't get a decent pot of jam. Strawberry and honey sounded very tempting.

– So what do we do now then, Missus?

– How do you know me name? And she started laughing again.

It stuck for the rest of their lives. He still called her Missus. Fifty years later there was still something of the stranger about her. Just some missus that stepped off a train into his cab.

When her wheezy laugh had run out of steam – he could have sworn blind it was a smoker's laugh – she didn't open the door to get out, or give him any new instructions, but just sat there, like she was in the living room of her own house. He felt like he was being cheeky, bringing up the subject of where to go.

– That's what they told me. Dumbarton Road. Dennistoun. Or t'other way round.

She stated it like the problem was his.

– Who did?

– These friends of mine.

– Close, are they?

That laughter again, filling up the taxi like a window had been left open.

– They'd bloody better live there. I've been sending their Christmas cards there for ten years.

The row of cabs behind him started blasting their horns. He turned on the engine and moved the car slowly through a red light round the corner. There was something in that decision. Why not just tell her to stop wasting his time? Why go out of his way for a woman who didn't even know where she was going?

The boots finally removed, pyjamas and dressing gown on, she went off out to the loo. He quickly grabbed a handful of tissues to wipe his crotch and the tops of his legs. He'd had a bit of bleeding for a few days now and didn't want her to know. For a start she'd worry her head off. And anyway, he'd already had one operation down there and had no intention of having another. He stuffed the hankies smeared with blood into his pyjama pocket. She came back in and sat in front of the mirror to comb her hair like she'd done every night for the last forty-five years.

– You'll comb that hair out. He used to tell her.

– On the contrary. Combing preserves the hair. You're the one that'll be bald before you're fifty.

Turned out she was wrong. His hair was thicker than hers. But his was grey, and had been since well before fifty. Somehow the combing had helped her keep her colour, though. She wasn't exactly strawberry blonde anymore, but she wasn't grey either. The honey had turned to syrup – a bright thin silvery sheen that perfectly coated the shape of her head, the way their sons' hair did when they were about a year old. She used the brush they had bought for Simon, the first one, forty-six years ago, with soft bristles that straightened the single layer of hair without scratching the skull. Nowadays, all it took was one sweep of the brush over the head, and her hair was sorted. But she did it over and over again, as if her hair was still thick.

He'd never expected to see her old. Every morning in life he'd gone off in his cab fully expecting her to be gone by the time he got back. She walked into his life in cardigan and slippers and might just as easily walk out of it.

– You just went into the station and got on the first train? He had turned round in the driver's seat to talk to her.

– Don't be daft. The first train out would've taken me straight back to Chorley. I'd just got off the bus from there. Anyway, Glasgow seemed just right. All those nice Scottish people. And then there was Molly and Jim.

– Dumbarton Road, Dennistoun?

– Or t'other way round.

– Molly and Jim what?

– Macdonald. Think you can find them?

– You must be joking. Everyone here's called Molly and Jim Macdonald.

– So what now?

He knew it should really have been him asking *her* that. He suggested an hotel, but she'd barely enough money on her for the hire out to Dennistoun. He suggested she go to the police and try and locate the Macdonalds, but she didn't like that idea at all. He wondered if she was on the run.

– Yeh. The Great Escape.

– Who from?

– Me old man. I didn't mean to, like. I just upped and offed, before he got home. I was sitting down to do my Christmas cards . . .

– In January?

– Better late than never.

For the next forty years they made a point of sending out their Christmas cards in January, as a kind of celebration. Some years it got even later. She thought you couldn't send out cards until there was snow – it was really the snow – she was celebrating. Once, their cards didn't go out until the end of February. This year, she hadn't worked up the energy for it at all yet. It was nearly March now. He had written, addressed and stamped the cards back in December, and was still waiting for her to post them. The fact that she hadn't, worried him. Maybe this was it. The signal. He would find her one of these days hobbling out the door in her slippers and elasticated trousers. He bought her a Damart body stocking, just in case. Not that he wanted her to go, but he didn't want her catching her death either.

In the taxi cab, she'd laid her head back against the window and closed her eyes.

– I'd had enough.

– Of what?

– Don't know rightly. Albert's a gent. Nothing he wouldn't do for me. Works hard, and buys me everything I want. Bought me one of those new Hoovers. First house in the street to have one. Works a treat too. But this morning I took the Hoover and hawked it round the neighbours. Got enough for the bus to Preston, and a ticket to here.

He could see poor Albert getting in from work, finding his wife and Hoover gone. Maybe he never found out she sold it, imagined his wife and Hoover rambling round the country together, leaving him alone in an empty house with dirty carpets.

He never bought her a Hoover. Not even when they became vacuum cleaners and everybody had one. They beat their carpets, hung them out the back, like in the old days. The boys never noticed, until they got married. Then their wives made them see that a house without a proper carpet cleaner is not a home. The girls didn't like their mother-in-law. Thought she neglected her motherly duties. In a way, it kind of kept the family together. The four wives, who had nothing else in common, ganged up, meeting regularly to discuss her shortcomings and how to make up for her to their menfolk. She never noticed. She wasn't what you'd call a woman's woman. It was only when Eddie, their second, split up with his wife that she took the slightest notice of any of her daughters-in-law. She sent her a letter with her birthday card every year, and another with the Christmas card.

He'd started up the engine.

– Where are we going?

– I'll see you all right for the night, at least.

She started to open the door as the car moved off.

– You've got it wrong, mister. I'm not in the market for hows-yer-father.

He stamped on the accelerator, pissed off at that and thought if she wants to jump, let her. But she closed the door again.

– I'm taking you to my sister's. She'll put you up. But you'll have to give her a sob story. Tell her your old man was thumping you or something. She likes a sad story, does Meg.

Meg died twenty-two years ago last June, and it was almost a relief. She'd been coming round to their house at least twice a week for over twenty-five years, just to make sure he wasn't thumping her. If Missus strained her ankle or whatever, Meg'd ask for all the details. If she jabbed herself on a thorn when she was out in the back doing the rose bushes, Meg looked in the sink and the cutlery drawer for a fork or a skewer with dried blood on it. Whenever he got fed up with it he'd shout a bit. Not at Meg, at her. Then she'd remind him the whole cock-and-bull story about her being bashed up was his idea in the first place.

The brushing routine finished, he helped her off with her dressing gown and into bed. He pulled the duvet back and held her hand to help her balance as she moved first one leg, then the other on to the bed, and sunk her frail body slowly down on to the sheet. Now they would talk, like they always did.

He'd tried his best never to let their lives get into routines, but with hindsight he had to admit they were riddled with them. Like talking before going to sleep. Every night since they were married, she would ask him about all the places he had been that day, and he would recount his tales, like an explorer back from the North Pole. He told her about the corners of the city he had poked about in in his little black cab, reeling off destinations like a Willy Nelson song: Ruchazie, Arden, Whitecraigs, Shettleston.

Until not so long back, the talking came after sex. Even in their seventies, they had managed a regular session. But it had eventually become a strain on their memories – each of them making love to the bodies they used to have – and on their tired limbs. She never said anything, but he realised how painful any kind of movement was becoming for her. Her moaning began to sound different. He stopped hearing the grunts of pleasure and the slap of spare flesh, and heard instead the scrape and whine of bone and pain. Anyway, his op had put paid to any inclinations in that direction.

So now they just lay side by side, in a way that, if anyone had come in the room, it would have looked like they had just been doing it. She stroked the hair on his chest, as she had always done, and he told her about the day's adventures. Not cabbying any more, of course. He had to retire at 65. But he still drove, taking the grandkids here and there, or just driving around. He sought out streets he had never been hired to go to. He thought if he kept on driving, he might stop himself turning into Albert; coming in at regular times, expecting to find her there, and then one day coming back to an empty house.

He never met Albert. And she never mentioned him. Except once when she had to file for a divorce before they could get married, and he had to sign a paper in a lawyer's office, stating that he had had an adulterous affair with Mrs

Albert Critchly. Some hope. It had been two years since she stepped into his taxi, and he'd got no more out of her than French kissing. It took another two years before they got married. But poor Albert must have sat appalled in his house in Chorley, his wife running round the country with his Hoover, having it off with Scotsmen.

Her pain was bad tonight. She didn't have to say anything. Grimace or moan or anything like that. He just knew it was bad. She couldn't prop herself up on her elbow any more to face him when they were talking. She lay flat on her back, with her head turned towards him, smiling. Even the smile hurt. He could tell.

– You want a rubbing?

He leaned over her to get her Tupperware box full of medicines and ointments, but she shook her head and pushed his arm gently away. It was the pain, he knew that. But, still, she was quieter these days. More distant, lost in her own thoughts. He wondered if she was thinking it was time she went back and explained to poor old Albert Critchly. If he was still alive. He turned out the light, and lay thinking in the dark. There was nothing he could do to make her stay. If only she'd send the damned Christmas cards, he'd feel easier.

She wasn't sleeping either. The pain was keeping her awake. She didn't move, but her breathing didn't change rhythm. He wanted to ask her if she was all right, but she got fed up with him asking that. He lay facing away from her, imagining that if he turned he'd see that strawberry blonde woman in cardigan and slippers. She touched his arm, and it reminded him of when she'd leant forward and touched his back when he was driving her that first day to Meg's.

– Thanks, love. She'd said. – See? I knew I could depend on you nice Scottish folk.

Her fingers on his back had felt warm despite the cold. Now they were cold against his arm, even though the heating was up full blast.

– You really want to know why I left? she said. Out of the blue, picking up a conversation started in a taxi half a century ago.

– There was no point in being there. Albert and Vera. The Critchlys, 14 Pendle Street, Chorley. Like Jim and Molly Macdonald. Too many of them.

– And here? John and Vera Murdoch, Ivanhoe Terrace, Cumbernauld?

– That's what I'm saying. I shouldn't be here. What am I doing being called Murdoch? I should never've got on that train. Shouldn't have sold that nice Hoover.

She coughed and laughed, squeezed his arm and turned around, settling into sleep.

The next morning, he woke. As usual, she'd got up before him and brought them both a cup of tea which they never drank. It was snowing outside. Well, sleeting. Big grey flecks of shredded cloud slid down the window pane. He reached out for his cuppa, and nudged her as she lay, still there and grinning that smoky grin of hers, beside him.

– Tea's getting cold, Missus.

He nudged her again, but she was gone.

Trials By Ordeal

Part 1: Oral

She checked the mantelpiece – the fifty pound note was still there. So were the pound coins, her credit card, and the Azteca earrings. He wasn't a thief. She hadn't really taken him for one. Clare knew thieves. They had a way of looking straight at you but widening their focus to see around you. They didn't glance away, that would be too telling. The thief's pupils dilated slightly, switching to fish lens in front of you, scanning the room in peripheral vision. She learnt that from watching Stevie.

Nor was he a drinker. Not a serious one. He'd only opened two of the cans she'd got in for him, and hadn't finished either of them. When she went to throw them out, about a quarter of each tin fizzed down her arms filling the room with the unfamiliar smell of moderation. A real drinker might have managed to keep it down to a couple of cans, coast for a while on the anticipation of the real drink he'd get when he got home. But leave cans unfinished?

All in all, ten out of ten. 'Course, he might've just been on his best behaviour. The very fact he *had* a best behaviour was something. Stevie would probably have had the sense to leave the fifty spot alone too, but the coins and the jewellery would have gone. And Stevie would have arrived half scooped. Brian had remained sober all night, kept picking up the coins and putting them into little bundles on the coffee table. Even when she wasn't in the room – she'd watched him through a chink in the door, pretending she'd gone to the loo. Maybe he suspected something. Even so. No test could ever be absolutely conclusive. He had passed. She'd have to accept the results. It'd be madness not to.

Getting ready for bed, she thought: if only she'd been this methodical when she first met Stevie. She wasn't going to be caught out again. Whatever happened this time around, she was on a winner. Either this Brian guy would turn out to be Mr. Right or Mr. Bastard – difference was, this time she'd spot it early on and give him a body swerve. She went over the questionnaire she'd put to Brian when he arrived. He'd said hello and then

– What d'you fancy doing, then?

And she'd said, hold on, she didn't know that much about him yet.

– Do you have any unappealing habits?

– Like what?

– Oh, I don't know. Pick your nose, poke your ears, scratch your bum?

–

– Sexual preferences?

– Just the usual. I think.

– Perversions?

– Other than going out with difficult women?

– Smoke?

– No.

– Drink?

– A bit.

– How big a bit?

– Not much.

– Write the first thing that comes into your head here.

She handed him an A4 sheet and a pen. Up to now he'd handled it pretty coolly. Mhairi must have briefed him well. This threw him a bit though.

– Standard psychological test. You can tell a lot about a man from his handwriting.

He'd got it now, and sat down happily and scribbled for a minute. Then handed it back.

– 'I like a challenge. Come out with me'. Left-to-right slope – ambitious, sure of yourself. Even spacing – reliable. Not sure about the wee smiling faces inside the O's but. Okay. Can I get you something to drink?

She stretched out in the bed, liking the idea that she needn't have been lying here alone if she didn't want to. There was a moment, a split second back there, when she'd almost taken him into the bedroom. He'd been kissing her politely, running his tongue round her lips but not pushing it into her mouth. She'd liked that. It was kind of friendly, like maybe there was some European or Eskimo nation somewhere that didn't kiss cheeks or rub noses, but ran the tips of their tongues quickly and unobtrusively round each others' lips. Like a mother might lick excess ice-cream from a child's mouth. She'd had this sudden urge to take him into the bedroom just to show him her gratitude. Thankfully, she'd stopped herself in time. Apart from anything else, it would have screwed up her system.

She looked down at her red bra and knickers. Somebody – Mhairi? her mother? – had told her wearing red was empowering. Clare said no, that was yellow polka-dotted ties. An old boss from yonks ago had told her that. She'd been slagging him for how hideous his tie was and he smiled at her and explained all about power dressing. Crock of shit. Then her mother or Mhairi or someone told her that American lawyers advised their clients to wear red. They could turn an immediately recognisable serial killer, all lank hair and suspiciously stained coat and penis-hole eyes, into a likeable prime-time TV presenter just by adding a measured quantity of red. A muted carmine tie or vermilion waist coat would do the trick for any jury anywhere. There were pictures with the article that Mhairi – yeh, it was Mhairi, that was her kind of territory – that Mhairi had been reading, and honestly Clare, it worked. You'd accept a bunch of carnations from this guy in the street any day.

Clare didn't suit red. She had copper coloured hair; copper like an old two pence piece that'd spent too long in other people's pockets, been rubbed by too many sweaty fingers. (Stevie's opening one-liner: 'Are you a *natural* mousy brown?') Her skin was skin-coloured, the way Boots and Clearasil think everybody's skin should be and nobody's is except hers: porridgy pinky, like the label on a tin of Tesco's economy tomato soup. Stevie used to play Colour Me Beautiful with her. Her perfect match, he said, was the mutton in an uncooked mutton pie. Stevie was a scream.

So she wore her red secretly, like illegal weapons. Power frillies. She lay in the bed with them on and felt in control. She knew exactly how she was going to progress with Brian. She felt no fear of the outcome, whichever way it went. The sense of satisfaction at a good day's work became physical. (Stevie used to say she should come into the showers after Saturday football. That was when he had his best hard-ons, if he'd played well. She wondered if they all got them, the players. Standing around in open showers like a gantry of beer pumps. This must be what it feels like, sturdy and direct, the goal posts fully in sight.) Two more little tests to go, both of them already thought through and organised down to the tiniest detail, and then she'd know. Not for sure, but as sure as you could be. She felt a hardness in her legs, tautness in her tummy, like she'd been training. She rolled over, comfortable in her redness, considered masturbating the way she thought men do, or at least Stevie did, as a matter of course, a way of easing off the day's excitement. But she was well asleep before she could summon the interest.

Part 2: Investigation

– What are you doing?

– I told you. Washing my teddies.

Mhairi stood at the bathroom door, staring at the line of dolls and soft bears that hung on a washing line over the bath by their arms, legs, crotches. Clare was soaping the last one.

– I thought you meant *teddies*. As in teddies, basques, cami-knickers –

– Thongs, whips. No fear. I'm not one of your New Chicks. Only women in the world that can lie down Sylvia Kristel and get up in the morning Andrea Dworkin.

The idea that you can choose your friends, it's a nonsense. Friends are like anything else – they're just there. You can decide whether to have them or not, but you can't choose which ones you get; that's a given. God knows where Clare and Mhairi met. They weren't at school or anything together. Didn't work together. Never shared a flat. Mhairi was a part of Clare's life, like the flats or jobs you ended up in rather than actually having the wherewithal to select. They were friends, simple as that. They commented on each others' lives, like quality control inspectors. Off-Friends.

It was Mhairi who had set her up with Brian. Three months of lectures about how Clare shouldn't let men dictate her sense of self-esteem. That was all very well for Mhairi: blond, slim, nice accent, trainee physiotherapist. Three months of how we're all better off without men, then she goes and sets her up with Brian. Mhairi – half feminist, half Cilla Black.

– If this is what it takes you to get over that neanderthal Stevie. Brian's a decent guy. Even if he has got a Lambada.

– Lambretta. Or so he says.

Half the guys in Clare's tribe claimed a 125cc Sfera, or an original '58 Vespa, or a Malaguti in for revamping some-where. Yeh, sure. That's why they run around in a Honda SH Fifty, the naffest bike on earth. It was dead-cert insight into a guy's psyche if he lied about his wheels. Lie about that, and everything else about you will be half-fiction. Brian said he had a Lambretta, an SX 200 at that. Didn't bring it last night because, he said, he thought they'd be going out and he'd be drinking. It was decided Mhairi should head up the Truthfulness Test. That way, they could do a double-check. She'd flirt with him a bit – after all it was originally Mhairi he'd fancied – and then see if he'd report *that* back to Clare (a spin-off being it was a good prelude to the final and biggest test still to come). And at the same time, of course, check on the size of his scooter.

– How the hell am *I* going to know the difference if it's a Lambretta or not?

Mhairi was nosing about inside Clare's wardrobe. She always did this, and Clare raked about in Mhairi's when she was over at her place. It was a form of tourism, excursions into the bazaars and souks of foreign psychologies. Mhairi came across Clare's Walkman.

– Maybe I should take this?

– Good idea.

If Mhairi was to feign interest in wheels, she'd better show she'd been seduced by other elements of the scene. Otherwise, Brian'd smell a rat.

– So long as I don't have to listen to that stuff you listen to.

– You'll have to. The earphones are rubbish. You can hear a mile off what you're into.

Clare handed her a couple of cassettes – Madness, Bad Manners.

– Aw. Do me a favour.

Clare gave Mhairi her instructions. She'd know immediately by Brian's status in the tribe whether he had the decent Lambretta he said he had. He'd be king pin. She was to look out for the legend 'SX 200' on the bike, which would be longer and sleeker than any of the others. Clare didn't know Brian's particular troop, him being from Ayr (Mhairi had met him at some trainee physiotherapists' convention in Irvine). But she'd seen them on trips down that way, cruising up and down the promenade. They were like any troop anywhere – except maybe the Southside Secret Scooters – most of them had bigger hats than bikes. *If*, like he claims, Brian did have a Lambretta 200 then he'd probably be the only one. The only other bike that might come close would be a Vespa. Smaller, rounder than the SX 200. To Clare's way of thinking a better machine all round, though that wasn't necessarily the accepted view. Unlikely there'd be a Vespa in the same league as Stevie's.

Or rather, Clare's. They'd gone halfers for it, but she'd picked the wrong moment to tell him he was a skunk-breath and to sling his hook. Stupidly, she'd waited till she'd got off the bike and he was still sitting on it. He rode off like Marlon Brando in The Wild One, except it was a scooter and it was on Duke Street and he's a skinny prat. As he went he yelled

– No more riding for you then, hen.

Mhairi was putting herself out here for Clare. She hated bikes, scooters more. Hated the Mod scene, the clothes, the music, the lot. Hated the guys, hated the girls. Why she liked Clare, or even if she liked her at all, Clare couldn't figure out. Whatever, Mhairi now saw herself as Clare's emotional consultant, a kind of personal management guru helping her recover from the recession of the Stevie years, limbering her up for the Brian boom. Like all consultants, you never dared ask why, if she was such an expert, she wasn't exactly rolling in the spondulicks of passion herself. Mhairi had hoped that, in the first stage of her rehabilitation, Clare would have given up the bikes and clothes and everything. Mhairi couldn't see that that would be too much of a climb down. And anyway, Clare still loved the scene.

There were Stevies everywhere you looked; they didn't all ride scooters. Clare was there first, before Stevie, before Brian. She had a bike when she was fifteen, an old Triumph Prima her Dad had bought her and fixed up for her. Pale green – Dad said to go with her lovely chestnut hair. She used to believe it, too. Thought she looked neat on that wee scooter. She loved it, didn't mind about the slagging Primas attracted. Christ, half the people who slagged her didn't even have wheels. She should never have let Stevie talk her into selling it to buy the Vespa between them. Now he'd pissed off with it. Maybe she could talk Brian – he was dopey enough – into selling his SX, if he had one, and get a new model. Then she'd piss off with his.

She stood at the kitchen window and watched Mhairi breeze gaily down the street, Clare's anorak too wee for her. A bad last-minute decision, that. She looked all wrong. They wouldn't fall for it. They'd spot her for an infiltrator a mile away. Clare went back to the bedroom, uneasy with the whole plan, put on Mhairi's Marks & Spencer's wool coat, and went out to check on Stevie.

Stevie had moved tribes. With a split new Vespa, hand-painted black by Clare with a Nightbreeder motif, the Southside Secret Scooters had laid out the red carpet for him. Now he was in with the top brass, riding alongside the buzziest of machines: souped-up Triumphs with new engines and Harley Davidson handle bars, elongated stretch-scooters, big boxy Metropolises. You name it. No doubt they'd have discovered by now that Stevie's a nob-head.

Everybody thinks Stevie's a nob-head. Clare did, even when she was going out with him. It was what she really needed at the time though, a nob-head. She'd been comfortable with him, comfortable with his insults, felt nice and snug with his drinking, his stealing from her, his pathetic leching after her friends. For a while she enjoyed behaving badly with him, effing and blinding with him, wallowing in his spasmodic scrubby sex. It was like burning your gums with alcohol to override a constant toothache.

VT! A VESPA'S FOR CHRISTMAS. CAF. MOD. SAT. BOD. OR YOU'LL ALWAYS WALK ALONE. NIGHTBREEDER.

Every month without fail, since they'd split up, Stevie'd been wooing her back in his inimitable style via the personal columns of *Scooter World*. VT stood for Vinegar Tits, Stevie's pet name for her. Every month, a variation on the same appeal – that she bring her body round to the Cafe Moderne on Saturday morning, their old haunt and meeting time. Today, she decided to go. Just to make absolutely sure that he wouldn't take himself off on a trip down to Ayr and blow Mhairi's cover.

Clare reckoned that Stevie reckoned that so long as he was in possession of the Vespa, he was still in with a shout with her. That was the saddest thing: Stevie loved her.

Seriously. That's why he held on to the bike, why he kept daring her to come and get it. Why she couldn't.

They sat at the back of the cafe. When she'd walked in he jangled the Vespa keys at her, then stuffed them down the front of his trousers. Seeing him again after so long, she saw he was better-looking than Brian, more regular features, thicker, darker hair. Better dresser too, in his Blitz checks and straight-legs, McKenzie boots as buckled as his face. But he was working hard to keep it up, harder than he used to. She wasn't going to tell him about Brian, then decided she might at least get some fun out of the whole situation. She told him Brian was a bit of a twat which was a great improvement on Stevie. When she was sure he wouldn't have the time now to take a trip to Ayr, she left, making the usual threats about lawyers' letters and getting the bike back. She almost felt sorry for him, he was that deflated when she just upped and offed.

The whole city looked disappointed, as if something that should have happened, hadn't. Everyone avoided everybody else's eyes trying to look as though *they* hadn't been expecting anything. They were getting on with things. Old guys who'd given up waiting, women who just looked glad nothing *had* happened, studenty types who tried to look as they didn't care if anything ever happened or not. She felt her skin like packaging around her, clingfilming her from the street, the shops, the passers-by, the spits of rain. She was being slow-cooked, wrapped in skin-foil and immersed in the slow heat of the dank city, her insides gradually congealing into a dark mass. Soon she'd be like the rest of them. Felt she already was, with this coat of Mhairi's on.

Back at the flat, Mhairi was waiting outside the door for her. She had tied her hair up in a high pony tail off the crown of her head and was chewing gum. It was that worst of all possible combinations – a lifetime's practised sweetness trying to be hard. Like those ministers at school who described themselves as with-it, wore their hair a dangerous two inches over their dog collar, played ten-year-old pop songs (He loves you yeah yeah yeah, God loves you yeah yeah yeah) and expected everyone to be impressed.

– He really is a nice guy, Clare. You're on a winner. If I were you I'd go get him.

– He has got a Lambretta then?

– I think so. A big thing, anyway. Everyone else was looking at it. It was yellow. Are Lambrettas yellow?

Mhairi liked that kind of remark. She sat down and watched as Clare dialled Brian's number. Clare put down the phone before it had time to ring out.

– Can't be arsed now.

– Do it! Come on. I want to see if he passes the test. He will. I promise. Have courage.

She dialled again, and Brian said all the right things. Gave her the news that that friend of hers – Mhairi, the one that'd introduced them – had passed by. She was getting into scooters. Clare must be doing a good PR job there, he'd never have taken Mhairi for the type. Even mentioned that she was coming on to him a bit. Said he just laughed it off. Admitted she was a looker, all the same.

– See? said Mhairi when Clare had hung up. – No way he'd say that to you if he was thinking of doing the dirty. He's really into you, Clare. He's gen. Perfect for you.

– Says he gave you a ride.

– Just round the block.

– In the tribe, that's foreplay.

– No no no. It's you he's after. Talked about you all the time. His little livewire.

They all thought that. That she was a livewire, Clare. Except sometimes for no reason, like today, she couldn't keep it up.

– I think we'll call it a day on the tests. Clearly, Brian is every girl's dream.

– No. I think you should go ahead with the last one, Clare. The biggie. After what Stevie did to you, you need to be sure. Anyway, it's all set up.

Part 3: Endurance

Actually, the set-up wasn't brilliant, but it would do. Brian comes round, finds Mhairi there instead of Clare. Mhairi gives him the story about Clare being suddenly called away: some family crisis in Paisley; she gets Mhairi to come over and wait for him. Mhairi tells him Clare won't be back tonight. Mhairi gets him inside, keeps him there by asking all about scooters and the scene. Maybe slags Clare off a bit. See how he reacts. Makes it plain she's up for a spot of illicit passion.

Clare was committed to the idea last week when she thought it up. Attractive girl, an acquaintance even, alone in flat; girlfriend certain not to turn up. Attractive girl lays it on a platter for him. How does boyfriend react? Should send the idea off to Terry Wogan.

Now she wasn't so sure, though. She began to see the flaws in the plan. Watching Mhairi scurrying around the guddle of the flat getting ready for the show all gung-ho for Brian to pass, it dawned on her that she herself actually wanted him to fail. Opposing objectives were hardly conducive to proper scientific research. Still, when Brian rang the door-bell, she went ahead and shut herself up in the wardrobe to peer out at the proceedings through the louvre slats. Brian had come in after a respectable degree of reticence, and then the next flaw made itself evident.

She should never have told Stevie about Brian. That's all

she needed, Stevie turning up here and finding her best mate half way to shagging her new pull. A scoop for *Scooter* magazine personal page. Or worse, Stevie turning up and reckoning with infallible logic that any lassie laying it on a platter for Brian was open to all offers. Stevie hardly knew Mhairi but he had made the incontrovertible assessment that under that modest and thinky veneer she was howling for it. He used to plead with Clare to call her over. He believed all those letters in *Rustler* and Readers' Wives and the ads looking for broadminded couples. It was just a bastard he happened to be surrounded by a bunch of boring girlies in this dead town.

Mhairi was being a bit literal. You couldn't fault her. She was doing just as Clare had instructed, asking endless questions about Lambrettas and Vespas and Blur and Oasis. She was doing an impressive job of looking interested. Brian was turning out to be a scooter and band bore. But there was something wrong about Mhairi's approach. Her interest was looking like real interest. She was smiling and nodding, not making eye contact, leaning forward in her seat, arms crossed on her lap. All wrong. None of this was saying let's do illegal acts. It was saying I'm a sweet girl, I'm sorry to be troubling you with so many questions when you'd really like to be with your girlfriend right now. She was acting like maybe she really did like him, didn't want to look like a slag in front of him. Come on, Mhairi, go for it; just get the damn thing over with, then everyone gets to go home early.

Eventually, Mhairi managed to get Brian out the room, asking him if he'd make some coffee.

– What are you playing at? Clare whispered when he was gone. – You're supposed to be telling him you're here for the bonking, not to start a discussion group.

– What do you suggest?

– Tell him outright. I want rogered. Show him your knickers.

– You must be joking.

– What is it to you what he thinks?

Mhairi was wearing a long skirt with buttons up the side. Clare got down on her knees and started undoing them.

– Whoah! What're you *doing*!

– Easy access. Don't panic. There's no risk. Just get him to make a move and then chuck him out. Five minutes max.

When he got back, Brian had thought the situation through, and had decided Mhairi couldn't be well. He was very gentle with her, but clearly he'd do anything to get out of there; felt he couldn't leave the poor woman on her own. Mhairi tried sticking her leg out of her opened-up skirt. It looked ridiculous, like she was about to show him her varicose veins or a new varuca. She leaned towards him, presumably in an attempt to seduce him into a kiss; instead she looked like she was going to fall over. Brian drew his body back from her, and at the same time stuck his arm out in case she needed support. He was getting seriously spooked.

All this was Stevie's fault. He was the reason Clare was entombed in her own cupboard, spying through greasy slats at her best friend martyring herself for her. She saw herself like in a vision, standing on a snakepit of shoelaces and belts and braces and shoulderstraps, entangled by the disembodied arms of shirts and anoraks. A grotesque Madonna in a Mod agony.

Mhairi had got herself into an impossible position. Perched on one buttock so she could stick her leg out as far as possible, stroking the leg unconvincingly with her left hand while her right hand was round her back clutching the skirt to make sure it wouldn't ride up that vital last half inch.

Brian was still freaked, but his expression had changed. Clare saw his face clearly for the first time when he changed position. He liked her. Brian liked *her*, Mhairi! Not the act, not the come-on – he hadn't a scooby that it *was* a come-on for chrissakes. He just liked her. Time to come out. She must make the effort, free herself from all this junk and just STEP OUT

Mhairi heard her move in the wardrobe and made one last reckless attempt to make a success of her mission. She lunged at Brian's trousers and grabbed his belt. He jerked back, astounded. Too terrified to stop her, she jiggled with his buckle like a maniac. Clare fell out of the cupboard just as Mhairi opened him up.

Mhairi looked at Brian. Brian looked at Clare. She thought he had stopped breathing. Mhairi collapsed, exhausted, in heap on the floor. Clare hadn't considered what she would do when she made her appearance. What should she say?

– Hi.

The Results

The first time she ever saw Stevie he was with Jodie. A dumpy wee thing who only pretended to be into wheels to get off with him. Stevie later explained that though he could easily get off with decent-looking lassies he thought ugly ones would be more likely to drop them. He said that was why, though he really fancied Clare, he hadn't hit on her. He thought she was too classy. Sure.

The last time she'd ever seen Stevie she was stepping out of a cupboard when she should have been in Paisley. Her new boyfriend's standing there stunned and her best friend's heaped on the floor having just made a lunge at his trousers.

Poor guy, thinks he's seen it all, when Stevie bursts through the door, screaming the odds and calling him a pervert. Stevie makes a dash at him and Clare sees her moment, grabs his keys out of his hand and makes a run for it, leaving Brian to his nightmare vision.

The Vespa sighed at her when she switched the ignition, like a pet dog returning home from kennels. She looked up at her window. Brian and Mhairi were clutched together, wide-eyed and open-mouthed. Stevie was running out the close behind her, squealing at her to come back, that he loves her. Clare leaves him behind, riding off down Alison street, without a helmet, her brown hair in her eyes like muddy splashback. Zip down the coast road for a bit, belt out into the empty night all the songs she could remember from *The Best of Bad Manners*, then home. By then, they'd all be gone.

Whispers

It was like walking through a forest of whispers. You'd be right there next to me, right at my side, and the whispers would be all around you, brushing your face, and you'd never mention them. I never knew where they came from or made out what they said, but they were always there. In the Arcade, in big shops or in crowded streets. At first I thought they were just the babble of ordinary voices. But they weren't. The whispers came from some dark place and belonged purely to you, clustering around your head alone, ignoring everyone but you.

You thought I couldn't hear them, so I pretended I didn't and said nothing. Then one day we were walking back to school after lunch. You had your head buried in a comic but you never bumped into anyone. We crossed the road at Shawlands Cross, and you still didn't look up. The cars whipped past all around avoiding you in favour of me. Then I knew these whispers of yours must be angels' voices, protecting you. *Our* angels never did anything useful like that. They got dished up all those prayers at Assembly every morning, which you didn't have to go to, but they couldn't even be bothered to help us up Pollokshaws Rd at lunctime.

I was jealous. So I made up the story about the dreams. Do you remember that first night round at my place, Nadjme? Mine was the only house in the street that had an upstairs, though it might as well not have had, because it was all closed up. Mum and Dad spent most of their lives living in a smaller and smaller space, abandoning rooms as soon as they became too cluttered to move in. You wanted to know what was in the rooms, and I told you how Dad had kept them locked since his shop closed, but that I could dream my way into them. I made that up on the spur of the moment, in case you thought there was nothing special about me at all. You weren't the least bit surprised, which only went to prove that such things were run of the mill to you. The problem was filling the rooms for you with more than just old boxes, so I stuffed them all with Dad's stories of the shop when it was a proper tobacconists. I told you there were important documents from all over the world, from Cuba and Virginia and Kenya and China. That there were boxes of cigars with pretty pictures on them and strange names – you made me write them down in your jotter – Schimmelpennick, Romeo and Juliet, Passing Cloud, any strange names I'd heard my Dad talk about. I put a glass case in the corner of one room and filled it with brittle brown leaves that Dad said Spanish girls used to roll on their thighs to make cigarettes. And I filled each room with the smell of a different kind of smoke: Havana, Sobrano, Turkish. I even described all those smells to you even though I'd never smelled them myself. Dad would have been proud of me.

At school the next day you brought in that big book. It was raining at morning break and we sat in a room by ourselves. The girls' common room had been taken over by your brothers and their friends for weeks because the white boys wouldn't let them in theirs. The teachers turned a blind eye to that because it avoided trouble. Ferguson (remember her? with her one deaf ear that I got wrong and got sent home for calling her Fanny?) thought you were being a nuisance when you asked for another room because the boys wouldn't give us peace to read.

I can still hear your voice, Nadjme – soft consonants on hard vowels, like a wave flowing over pebbles – translating the beautiful squiggles in that book, tracing your finger along the lines the wrong way round, from right to left. You were sure no-one gets to inhale the fumes of four continents without there being a reason for it, and that there must be some kind of holiness in these smoky dreams. We searched that book for a lost soul or an angel who might be behind it all. (We never bothered looking up the holy books in school because we thought Christian angels would probably be anti-smoking.)

By the end of the day, we still hadn't found a suitable candidate but I knew that the whispers would give you the answer as we walked home. We passed that man we used to see every evening on the way home from school. He lived on a small patch of muddy grass where a tenement had been bombed during the war. I always wanted to cross the street, but you said that was wrong of me and made a point of smiling over at him and waving. The old man never waved back. I know now that his world only went as far as the edge of the grass and no further. Your daily wave was an invasion from a foreign country. That's what people did when they grew up. They made a small space for themselves, the smaller the better. Your Mum set her boundaries by only speaking in a foreign language; my Mum and Dad used the remnants of a shop that had been closed for years, and weighted us down with cardboard boxes as ballast.

We got as far as Presto in the shopping centre, your head still buried in the book, when you stopped dead and squealed you'd found her. I still remember her name (I was surprised it was a she – I didn't think you could get lady angels): the Princess Al 'Uzzat. A jinnee you called her, and read out that she was one of God's Watchers at the Gate of Heaven, who only appear to us as shooting stars. Your voice sounded like a shooting star might sound if you were right up close to one: a hard glassy sound, so bright and clear that you could never hide anything behind it.

That's when all the tests and experiments began. If I had been given such a wonderful gift, it was my duty to work on it, you said, expand its power, increase my control over it. Sometimes I felt terribly guilty because I had made the whole thing up. I thought maybe I was committing a dreadful sin and would be punished for all eternity for it. But most of the time I forgot that none of it was true, and threw myself into the exercises you set me.

The first missions were easy. I had to report each morning with more details about what was in the locked rooms upstairs. Dad was always keen to talk about the old days in the tobacco shop, and then I'd go to bed full of his stories and really did dream about what might be hidden away up there. Getting out the house was more tricky: I lay in bed and concentrated as hard as I could on the sounds outside the window and imagined what the streets were like when they were dark and empty. I supplied you with dogs and cats, foxes sometimes, big men with knives, slaggy women, and you never questioned my shooting stars that fell to earth in a burst of light behind Safeway.

Does this pain you, Nadjme? That even me, your best

friend, made all this up, lied to you? You never doubted at the time. Even when I was sent to see the exam papers of the following day and came back with a list of questions which, in the event, never came up, you decided it was because the princess Al 'Uzzat would not allow my gift to be used for dishonest ends. At other times I was lucky, like when you sent me to your uncle's house. I reported back the next morning with vague descriptions of red furry wallpaper like I'd seen in your house, and threw in a dog barking for effect. You jumped up and down with excitement. Your uncle had waited all night for me and nothing had happened except that his dog suddenly started barking for no reason, looking up at the ceiling. You hadn't told me your uncle had a dog, so I couldn't have known that, and we held hands and skipped down the road, and sat in class all day ignoring the teacher, exchanging secret, happy glances with each other.

We were perfect together then. The others with their fighting and cat-calling in the yard were pathetic children, and we paid them no mind. You with your whispers sailing around you like tiny butterflies and me with my gift of seeing into shadows and locked rooms, set us above all the hassles at school. Those meetings when your Uncle shouted at my Dad, Fanny Ferguson telling us we'd be better not walking home together, the police outside the school gates – none of it had anything to do with us. We were too busy visiting Steven Grimes's and Robert Eadie's bedrooms. I told you that Steven – the love of your life – wore flowery pyjamas and that Robert – my choice of the 6th years – had hairs on his legs that went all the way up to his underpants. You thought that was disgusting, but asked if he took the pants off. I said no, because I'd no idea what I'd say if you asked me what he looked like without them. Wait and see if Steven takes his off next time, you said.

Do you still have the notebooks? All the entries you carefully noted down and then colour coded. Green for the locked rooms, wasn't it? Red for outside, blue for visits to other houses, black for selected boys' bedrooms (and sometimes teachers' bedrooms too, if we thought it'd be worth a laugh). It never dawned on us that the princess might have become angry with us for using her gift to spy into boys' rooms or make fun of teachers. But what do you think now, looking back, if you do look back in your new home so far away? Did we make her angry?

I had really begun to believe in her, Nadjme. Sometimes I thought I wasn't making things up, that I really had flown freely across the city and seen things she had allowed me to see. I was only thirteen. I still thought there was a connection between the way things were and the way I imagined them to be. I don't think that any more. And I don't believe in the princess any more, either.

I still dream, though. All the time, whether I want to or not. They tell me you live in a wide open space now, with mountains miles and miles away that seem to be just outside your door. Maybe that's what I see now when I close my eyes – huge shadows that, without your help, I don't understand. I live in my own small flat, twenty storeys up and with walls so thin that sometimes I think I can smell sweet sobrano drifting across the city from where we used to live. I try hard to dream my way to you, to tell you I'm sorry, that if I hadn't told so many lies our princess might have let me see what was happening that night.

The day after the fire, I heard for the first time what the whispers said. It was Saturday and we met as usual in the Arcade. You were very quiet, and your eyes and skin looked darker and angry. I was dying to tell you what I had dreamt the night before. This time the dream was real – I wouldn't have made that up, Nadjme. I saw shadows, like the ones

I've been seeing since, and the feeling of being somewhere not mine to be in. I was outside and it was dark. Then there was a flash of light, like when the shooting stars came out of the sky, and in the light I saw your house. Your brothers were at the windows (I never told you, but I used to try hardest to visit Imran's room at night) and I saw them all waving. I thought they were trying to tell me something.

But it was too late. The letter bomb had burnt down your door, and the fire had swallowed up the front of the house before it was put out. Then you told me you wouldn't be going back to school on Monday, because your father had decided to take you all away. A week later you were gone. I passed your house with my Dad and he said it was a terrible thing to have happened but it was probably for the best.

That day – the last day I saw you – you were in a bad mood, because I'd said the Princess Al 'Uzzat did exist and you said she didn't. We walked on, not knowing what to say to each other. I knew it would be the last time I'd hear them, so I concentrated hard on the whispers that puffed up around you as we passed the crowded shops. People pushed by us, a posh lady in a blue coat and a young man carrying a baby, a girl with a school uniform and a tennis racquet. We all turned our heads slightly away from one another the way you do when you're squeezing past, so I never saw anyone's lips move. But for the first time I heard the scattered whispers tuft delicately into words, and they said black bastard, paki and darkie cunt.

Rare Fish

Eh bien. Je

Now what? The future? Future imperfect? She checked
the phrase book. (They laughed, Pascal and Lucie and Harry,
at her and her phrase book: 'What's the point in giving you
the questions if you don't understand the answer?')
Voudrais. Conditional: I would like.

Je voudrais que

How many que's do you need? French likes to scatter
these little words around. Panache Harry, she told him,
softening the ch. She believed in writing to the French in
French. Oh not proper French, of course, how could she?
Mind you, she'd got by nicely enough in Brittany and
although they laughed she noticed how they *always* understood. And so what if Pascal and Lucie spoke perfect English
– *they* had to start somewhere, didn't they? If you're having

French people over then the least you can do is make the effort. Naturally the best Sarah could do was cobble together a few phrases with odds and sods of vocabulary half-remembered from schooldays. Just so long as they *understood*. Je voudrais que vous. Thank heaven she was writing to the two of them, no need to worry about tu or vous. Pascal had used the tu with her and vous for Harry, but Lucie called them both tu, all of which made life very confusing. The niceties of direct speech she would deal with when they arrived.

When they arrived. 'They're not taking us up on it, are they?' Harry said when Lucie's letter came. 'You don't expect anyone to take these invitations seriously.' It annoys Sarah that Harry has no taste for the unexpected.

'Aren't you pleased? Sarah was pleased. 'Take Pascal to the river. Tell him about fish.'

'Pascal's not interested in fish.'

Well, Sarah looked forward to it anyway. Sarah understands the value of getting to know foreigners. The Oxfam shop sent her on a course once and there were Africans there and Indians and that convinced her all the more how important it is to meet people from other cultures. Broadens the mind; makes you realise our lives are small. They're *meant* to be small. It's a big world and Harry and her are just part of it. Small lives make more sense in numbers.

She put the pen down and scattered some of Harry's special mixture into the fish tank. Andrew Possibly (The Last Surviving Vendace In Scotland) ate what he could and slipped shyly back down behind his rock, careful not to look Morag or any of her disdainful Arctic Charr family in the eye. 'Never you mind her, Andrew Possibly'. Sarah waved her pen at him. 'You wait till Harry brings Jane Certainly home for you. Then we'll see Morag smile on the other side of her face.' Andrew Possibly stared back at her. He'd been there a week now and had given up the search for another vendace in a world full of unfriendly charr. Now he only came up to eat, retreating behind his rock to wait and see if Harry ever would come up trumps. 'You wait and see.'

Eh bien. Je voudrais que vous + subjunctive. Hell. French Without Tears, Section 4: Verbs which introduce a Subjunctive Clause; A) Verbs of Wishing. If she was *really* honest with herself, what Sarah actually looked forward to was *having had* French people stay with them. (Try putting that in French, Andrew Possibly. What is it – pluperfect? Or is that just *had*?) Then her life would feel richer because she had made the effort and *had had* French people staying in her house.

Je voudrais que vous + present subjunctive. I would like you to come and see our beautiful country and meet our friends and try our traditional cooking which we told you about last year in Brittany. Pascal and Lucie thought there was no such thing as Scottish cooking. Harry got a bit miffed at that but Sarah understood what they meant: 'we haven't preserved our customs like they have, Harry'. Harry didn't think you went about saying things like that to foreigners. He said there *was* a healthy traditional cuisine, never for a moment thinking they might come over and see for themselves. Sarah phoned Christine to ask if she knew any recipes, but Christine said that what she ate in Edinburgh was thalis and Greek vegetarian and if you really want to be internationalist, Mum, then that's what you should be giving them.

C'est avec plaisir que j'attends notre rencontre. (Section 7: Writing Letters; phrase 10: I look forward to your visit.) De la semaine prochaine she managed by herself.

Time flies. Pascal and Lucie due tomorrow 'at 10.47, if your train timetables are to be relied upon. This allows for the 5 minutes in taxi you say it is to your house and another 5 minutes waiting time'. Lucie is *so* precise. Sarah had had a hectic week getting everything ready. Ideally she'd wanted Harry to go and meet them at the station, but they'd picked the worst possible time. The river would be in high spate the way it was when Harry found Andrew Possibly washed up in a rock pool. If Harry had any chance of finding Jane Certainly and reintroducing vendace to its home country, he would have to be there that morning and every morning of the spate. Which meant that all this week Sarah had to get back sharpish from the shop, see to Andrew Possibly, and then get on with the preparations for Pascal and Lucie.

She had planned their stay, Lucie-style, to the last detail. Day 1: Morning free, Afternoon Loch Lomond, Evening Meal (Cullen skink); Day 2: Princes' Square, Lunch out, Afternoon The Burrell, Evening Meal (Venison), Graham and Penny over for drinks; Day 3: Morning trip to Andrew Possibly's river, pub lunch, Afternoon free, Evening Meal (Herring in Oatmeal), then the Concert Hall (Popular Classics); Day 4: Edinburgh (Christine to organise lunch), Evening Meal (stovies).

Sarah poured Harry's slimy mixture ('plankton, dear') into the tank and gave Andrew Possibly a reassuring smile. He'd deteriorated over the last few days. Psychologically. They never should have talked about the Fish Trust's decision in front of him. One more week in captivity and if a mate hadn't been found, back went Andrew to continue the search on his own. Million-to-one-chance Harry said. Andrew Possibly cowered behind his little rock from Morag while Sarah wiped the slime from her hands. This is the worst bit: once they're here the time'll fly by, what with zipping about here and there, cooking and all. Then before you know it Pascal and Lucie'll be gone and it'll be lovely *having had* them.

'So what are they like, this Pascal and Lisa?' Christine had come home for the day to help out, though so far she'd spent most of it emptying her room to shift stuff over to Edinburgh.

'Lucie. Pascal and *Lucie*. Sarah worked hard at the u in Lucie. Purse the lips for u but say ee. When Lucie said it it sounded so elegant. When Sarah said it it sounded common. 'What are they like? Let's see. *He's* very quiet. A lawyer. You'd get on well with him. Lucie's more open. Very fussy. Everything organised down to the last detail. When we went on picnics she'd measure out the milk we'd need to the nearest centilitre. But it was a great holiday. We all got on very well.'

You couldn't really include Harry in that. Harry prefers fish. Pascal wandered around behind him as Harry dragged his net and dipped his snorkled head into little rivers. Pascal wasn't the least bit interested in Harry's fish; it was Harry who fascinated him. Now Harry doesn't like people to be fascinated by people, and he blamed Sarah for making friends with them and for two weeks he tried to shake Pascal off. Lucie and Sarah watched them, two little boys sizing each other up on the beach. The ebb and flow, the coming together and backing off. 'Très drôle Lucie, n'est ce pas?' Harry didn't speak to Sarah for a week after they'd returned.

'They're from Paris you know. You might get an invite.'

'Couldn't go Mum. Got to study.'

'What's French for Sociology? Sociolog*ie*?' Christine just laughed.

'*I* know how you all laugh at me. And I don't care. Lucie said to me at the end of the holiday she said, Sarah – *Sah-hra* – your French is improving. You see? You have to start somewhere.'

Day 3 and Sarah's plans are in a mess. Loch Lomond went well enough despite the weather, but Pascal had smiled weakly at the Cullen Skink which he said was very tasty but very filling and put his fork down after two mouthfuls. Lucie had managed a few more bites and then pushed her plate away – Sarah reckoned precisely two centimetres. And Harry was always funny about eating fish. Well, fish stews. Probably he was frightened that he might be chewing the last morsels of Jane Certainly. Princes Square got them out of the rain and Lucie bought a dress. Sarah said it's that nice, Lucie, you could nearly get away with wearing it in Paris. Par*ee*. They liked the Burrell but not the venison. Pascal said deer was an endangered species, despite Harry telling him this was farmed venison and anyway the country's full to bursting with them. Lucie inclined towards Pascal's argument and she pushed her plate an extra centimetre away. They would have given Graham and Penny the casting vote but Graham and Penny didn't turn up, so they went in to look at the fish tank instead. 'Funny name' said Lucie on being introduced to Andrew Possibly.

Sarah explained: 'Harry christened him Andrew the Last Surviving Vendace in Scotland, because they're supposed to be extinct here'. She turned to Harry and smiled. 'But I've high hopes that Harry'll find a Jane for him. So I call him Andrew Possibly'. Harry ignored her smile and said to Pascal: 'Course if I do find her, she'll certainly be the last vendace in Scotland'.

'But if you find her', the French added 'then they'll be the first of many vendace in Scotland'. Harry laughed, and all that went very well. Until Pascal said 'can you eat them?' which was when Harry began to worry that the French were building up to a Rare Fish Feast.

Next morning, while Lucie and Pascal debated whether it was a day for buttoning up the tops of anoraks or not, Sarah cried off from accompanying them to Andrew Possibly's river. 'Bloody Norah, Sarah,' Harry whispered outside the kitchen door. She whispered back: 'I've got to get them some French food or they'll starve to death.' 'Or eat my Arctic Charr,' Harry said and gave in.

Sarah spent the morning looking through cookbooks and coordinating bus journeys to the west-end delicatessens. When she got back the others hadn't appeared which gave her a chance to prepare the evening meal. Late afternoon a mournful trio arrive at the door.

'No, *Sah-hra*, really, we had a lovely time. Harry is so funny, no? He spends hours and hours looking into a little muddy river. He didn't even drink his coffee and now I have a whole quarter pint of milk left over.' Pascal said nothing and went up with Lucie to dry off.

'Really, Harry. They're soaked through.'

Harry went out. She could've cried if it hadn't been for the nice French meal she had all ready. She sat and waited quietly with Andrew Possibly, the two of them ignoring smug Morag and family ('just cause she's a little less rare than you') until she heard Harry come back in and then she shouted upstairs. 'Attention. Dejeuner.'

When they were all seated she came out of the kitchen triumphantly bearing broiled fresh endives served with spaghettis in tapenade and salade niçoise, and they all settled down to dinner and conversation during which Pascal asked Harry why he didn't keep tropical fish – angel fish, that sort of thing – which are more interesting.

'They are not. Rare fish are interesting. Charr and sparling and vendace are interesting. More people should keep them or they'll die out and all we'll be left with is Japanese things.'

'But it's only natural that things should die out, Harry, my friend. To make room for new things.'

The French meal didn't help either. Pascal and Lucie ate a little more than before, but never reached the half-way mark. Harry sat brooding and Sarah was on the verge of giving up when Lucie treated Sarah to a-whole-sentence-of-slowly-enunciated-French. '*Sah-hra*, you have been too kind to us already. So tomorrow, Pascal and I will make our meal. Oui?'

Yes! Thank God. And they all decided it had been a long day, best skip the concert and have an early night. 'What did she say?' said Harry before he went to sleep. Well, they're not cooking my fish. ('Don't be silly, dear'.)

Edinburgh went down well. Mainly because Harry didn't come. There was an extraordinary meeting of the Fish Trust. A decision had to be reached about Andrew Possibly. So Sarah followed Lucie and Pascal who in turn followed Christine around the galleries and museums. When she found a minute out of earshot of her guests she pleaded with Christine to come back with them for tonight's meal. One more night alone with them and your father'll cause an international incident.

When they got home they found Harry in the doldrums. The Trust had admonished him for taking the vendace out of its natural habitat and instructed him to return it at once. Harry told them that that meant almost certain death. Obviously the vendace had swum out of its normal range and had got lost. His chances of finding a mate alone were infinitesimal. Million-to-one. Well, they are now, Harry, they said. Sarah consoled him by saying you never know, maybe Jane Certainly'll turn up tomorrow. Then she threw together a tomato salad which was the only thing that had gone down well so far, while Pascal and Lucie went and did the shopping. Harry sat by the fish tank. Just in case.

Pascal and Lucie arrived with a small bag, and Sarah watched out of the corner of her eye, pretending to do the dishes, while they went to work. They brought out a family-size bag of Cadbury's Smash and two tins of beans. They carefully measured out exactly one and a quarter pints of water and half a pint of milk and added it to the Smash, deftly stirring the mixture in the pot. Then they heated the beans. Then they transferred the beans and the mashed potatoes on to four dishes: two of beans and two of potatoes. Then they set the table for two. Two glasses of water, two sets of cutlery. They set down one plate of beans and one plate of Smash at each place.

Then they sat down to eat, leaving Christine and Harry to pick at the tomato salad and Sarah to concentrate on her French, trying to keep the tears back again.

'Is that all you're having?' Lucie asked. 'Well, we have all been eating richly, haven't we?'

You and your French. Harry said that when they were getting into bed. Might as well have eaten the vendace. Which was when Sarah finally did burst into tears. 'Stop being silly, *Sah-hra*. You just don't understand French,' he said. 'Pity. The Smash looked good' and turned round and went to sleep.

Eh bien.

That was last night. Christine is back in Edinburgh and Harry's taking the Last Surviving Vendace in Scotland back to his river. Pascal and Lucie have gone home a day early. This is the good bit. She *had had* French guests to stay and all in all it had not gone too badly. She would tell them all about it next week at the shop. You'd never guess French people would eat Cadbury's Smash now, would you? She looks out the phrase book and leaves it beside the pen and paper on the kitchen table, and then goes to look at the empty space in the fish tank where Andrew used to be. She dips her hand into the tank and looking her straight in the eye – or as straight in the eye as you can with fish – she grabs the insolent Morag by the tail and carries her into the kitchen. She leaves her dancing on the work-top and returns to her letter. Duty before breakfast.

Eh bien nous had such a lovely time during your visit. Now what do I want for that, Morag? Past perfect?

The Mystery Of Sabina Vasiliev

You never appreciate the good things in life until they're gone. Like the Cold War. Of course, even that was a double-edged sword – if it hadn't been for the Cold War Matthew would never have met her, and all three of us would have avoided the whole messy business. But I miss it all the same.

I can just see the two of them, still now after all this time: Sabina's body like a secret, her nakedness a dark whisper. Even asleep, her body must have controlled the space around him. When she moved, her limbs would have disturbed the pale air in his room, like a warm breeze against his skin. He told me she never stayed the whole night, always getting up to go before dawn. I imagine he used to watch her dress, her clothes merely adding another sensual layer, like failed decoys attracting attention to the body they were supposed to conceal.

When they first met, he came running up to my office to tell me all about her, starting with her hair.

– Molten copper. Like it'd be hot to the touch – and worked down from there. Narrow Russian eyes. Lips like Natassja Kinski's. Walks like a gypsy (*Hungarian* gypsy if I remember right). Skin sallow as a Turk's.

– An amalgam of the East, he said, pacing the office in front of my desk. Naturally I was contemptuous of high-minded Matthew, naturally gloating over some woman he'd picked up through a lonely hearts ad. He explained this away with his usual sententious logic:

1: he had happened on the advert by chance;

2: she was Czech, over here perhaps for political reasons – Matthew as an ex-Party member was interested in Eastern Europe and in politics;

3: she needed help with her English – he was an English teacher. (She'd written: 'I am tall with a long brown hair' and Matthew replied wittily 'Where is it?').

The idea that she might be willing to offer him sex was never mentioned. However, I remembered, years ago, Matthew fantasizing about life in Czechoslovakia. He had this idea that all Czech women have these great big difficult books which they put under their backs so that they can do it in weird positions with the men, who, by the way, are all university professors except that they work as window cleaners. Naturally, the women had read the books first, Matthew not being in any way sexist. Anyway, they met (eventually – I suspect she tried out one or two other respondents first) and from that first meeting, Matthew's fantasy became flesh.

He was right about the politics, though. This was the tail end of '89, the Berlin Wall was being hacked away and the papers were predicting revolution any day in Czechoslovakia. When it finally came just before Christmas, it heralded the conclusion of the Cold War, and the end of Sabina. But that was a while away yet: there were several months of frenetic sexual activity to get through first. Sabina turned out to prefer touch to talk. Once – and Matthew told me this only after the final debacle, when he had lost any sense of loyalty towards her – she insisted on doing it on a crowded bus, presumably because it *was* a crowded bus. She slipped her knickers off; undid his fly and sat on his knee, and laughed at the look of alarm on his face. When he told me this it was as irrefutable proof of her badness, though I don't remember him complaining at the time. Before the Velvet Revolution he'd only ever hinted at what they got up to together, respecting her privacy by talking in purely abstract terms. It was a couple of months before I got to meet her, but when I did I found myself filling in the unspoken details.

She didn't like to talk about events in Prague. Only sometimes, in the quiet light of early mornings, sated, she would curl up with him, and reminisce a little about her family and home, as if they were in a safe house, protected for the moment from the world outside. And when the TV or radio covered the mounting unrest in her country she added a bit of background detail for Matthew's benefit. Her past was a kind of aphrodisiac for him (and, soon, for me too, although only Matthew was allowed beyond the political foreplay.) He was genuinely concerned about her status in this country, which is how I came to know so much about their affair. As well as confiding in me as a friend, Matthew sought my legal advice – particularly when they began talking about getting married.

Sabina never stayed the whole night at Matthew's and always refused to let him see her all the way home – the closest he got was the corner at the end of her street. For reasons she wouldn't discuss she said the fewer people who knew about Matthew, the better – at least until after the Revolution. We thought she was being a bit paranoid. This was Glasgow, for God's sake, not Prague or Havana. Glasgow isn't blessed with spies. Sabina laughed and said that's why they sent her here.

It was November before I finally got to meet her. The two of them had kept themselves isolated from everyone; constructed a kind of Warsaw Pact around their new-found freedom. But now, with the papers predicting an imminent and bloody battle in Czechoslovakia, Matthew wanted to get her legal status cleared up as quickly as possible. I agreed with him about her hair (you *don't* get that colour in the West) and everything else. Her thick accent, her attitudes, poses, unpredictability. Getting information out of her was not easy, especially as she tended to lapse mid-sentence into virtual foreplay with the preening Matthew. But I understood immediately that Sabina's freedom had been hard won, and therefore to be cherished and acted upon at all times – perhaps especially in public.

Matthew had set the meeting up in a pub, and it seemed strange to be sitting there talking in hushed voices of revolution and subversion off the back of Charing Cross. Perhaps it wouldn't have seemed so to people of my grandfather's age, but to me Charing Cross and revolution are mutually exclusive. This was the first of two conversations – though I saw her often in between – that I can still recall precisely, word for word. The second was in my office before she disappeared. In this first encounter I managed to leach slowly out of her the basic facts of how she came to be here. She was the daughter of a medium-level Party official. She had become involved with a *samizdat* magazine. There was a boyfriend, (Matthew feigned disinterest in him), Tomás, who during a routine police check, got jittery and landed his comrades and her in the shit. Her father helped her out, first to Berlin, where Jurgen (a short-term lover) helped her get into Britain. The Authorities – though *which* authorities I couldn't determine – knew of her presence here, but advised her not to seek legal status yet. All she could do was sit tight and wait for events in Prague to catch up.

I tried my best to get hard, legal information, but Sabina, homesick I suppose, spent most of the time talking dreamily about her home a few miles out of Prague in the Bohemian woodlands

– Between the River Laabe and the River Berounka. My mother called it the River's Kiss.

Everything about Sabina – her hair, the shape of her body, her accent – was impossibly East European, just as Matthew had said

– I used to sit in the stream that ran through the garden and let the water run down along my legs.

And:

– At night the trees reached out and rubbed against you so that even though you couldn't see anything because it was dark, you could *feel* that you were still alive.

She spoke, without much prompting, about Jurgen, but never about Tomás.

– We used to have to make love wherever we could, Jurgen and me. It was too dangerous for us to meet in the houses of the families who were hiding us.

She said that Jurgen and she always cried afterwards.

– Jurgen said we were really making love to ourselves. Or, perhaps, to the people we would like to be.

That first night I went home by bus. I was waiting at the bus stop feeling that if I stood there long enough and still enough, I would dissolve into the inscrutable stone of this city. Become fixed, unable to move. Earthed in this one spot forever. Then I saw her down the street with Matthew. She didn't look round. She was dancing around him, her voice thinning the night, and it was as though an unexpected harsh light had woken me from sleep.

I said there were two encounters that I can remember in perfect detail, and that's true. But there was a third which I can see so clearly in my mind's eye that I often find myself telling the story as if I had actually been present. Matthew came round to my house one night, excited. I was used to this by now, of course. A colleague of his – a Modern Studies Teacher, or some such – had asked if Sabina could come round and talk to his 6th years. History in the making, that sort of thing. He agreed to ask Sabina, and surprisingly, she'd agreed. Naturally, Sabina wowed the kids. Well, I said, it *is* an all-boys' school.

– No. Not that. Well that, too, but what she did was, she went up to the blackboard and drew a cross at the top right-hand side. She says, 'this is Franz Joseph Island, in Russia, right?' 'And over here', and she drew a cross on the left-hand side, 'this is Iceland'. Then at the bottom of the board she marked out Crete to the east and the Azores to the west. Then she says to the boys, 'that's the four corners of Europe, right?'

– Not necessarily, I said, and Matthew agreed that any definition of Europe by geographical or cultural frontiers was a dangerous business.

– But listen to this, he went on. – *If* we take these as four possible corners of Europe, Sabina asked the boys where they thought the centre of Europe would lie? They're an eager lot, 6A, and a few of them took pretty reasonable stabs at it. Berlin. Vienna, et cetera. You're the lawyer – he leaned over towards me, eyes bright with the answer. – Where do *you* think it lies?

It seemed pretty obvious to me.

– Prague, I imagine.

– Nope, says Matthew. – Motherwell. I checked it. To be

absolutely accurate, on my atlas at home the very centre of Europe lies two miles south-east of Motherwell. Craigneuk, in fact. Craigneuk is the *epicentre* of Europe!

I've tried this out a few times myself since and each time the centre of my cross falls in the ocean, but to be fair, the nearest country is indeed Scotland. Matthew told me how this discovery really woke his boys up, made them feel at the heart of things. But they weren't nearly as turned on as Matthew was. Everything he had always longed for had come true for him – the love of a notorious, sexy woman and being suddenly thrown into the boiling pot of political events. Sabina and he went public and soon they were celebrated around the bars and coffee-shops of the west end. Wherever they went, they were surrounded by people trying to get closer to the magical Sabina and hoping that some of Matthew's luck would rub off on them. For my part, I stayed away as much as I could. I, too, wanted to be near Sabina, but I resented sharing her with all these hangers-on. And, worse, with Matthew himself.

My hopes for replacing Matthew in Sabina's affections were given an unexpected boost by Sabina's cooling off on the prospect of getting married. While Matthew tried to organise his side of a things – registry office, church (both of them were born Catholic), suggesting dates – Sabina made it obvious that her position here, unrecognised by her own State, made the possibility of marriage hopeless. Nor did I try very hard to find a way around the problem, despite Matthew's pleadings for advice. However, I know now, in the light of what she was just about to tell me that her stalling was not on account of her not loving Matthew. She loved him all right. Completely. No doubt still does, which makes his behaviour now all the more criminal.

There were demonstrations on the streets of Prague and Bratislava in late November, with scenes of crowds protesting in thick snow on the TV. Everyone expected bloodshed. On the other side of the Continent Sabina Vasiliev walked into my office, alone for the first time. Even cold wars are interruptions in peoples' lives, opportunities to live differently in the chaos. But once the battle is won or lost, partnerships founded on the struggle fall apart. Sabina genuinely wanted victory for the people of Eastern Europe, but the continuation of the brutal regime in Prague would have suited her own circumstances better. Public victory, private defeat.

– I didn't think we'd fall in love. If I'd meant that, I'd never have done it.

Her accent was thicker than ever. She settled into the chair in front of my desk, composed and resolved, rested her hands, lightly clasped, on her lap. She didn't flinch from that position for twenty minutes until she'd finished what she had to say. Then she got up and walked out of my office, sad and dignified. I never saw Sabina Vasiliev again.

– My name is not Sabina Vasiliev. I have no connection with Czechoslovakia, except for a friend I knew called Tereza who taught me a little Czech. I used her story. My name is Sandra Hamilton. My mother is dead and my father drinks. I bring up my younger brothers myself. I get bored.

– Years ago, a group of us used to go out at night and pretend we were foreign. People are more interested in you if you're foreign. My friends all stopped doing it after a while, but I didn't. I went on pretending to be Italian, Australian, whatever. Then I discovered Sabina and she fitted me like a glove. Sandra Hamilton is a much harder part to play. Why should I be Sandra? I don't feel like her. She belongs to other people. Sabina belongs to me. She's got her own life, because I breathe it into her. I've been Sabina for so long now I find it hard to be anyone else.

– I knew Matthew before I became Sabina. He was a

couple of years up the school from me. I always liked him. He doesn't remember me. I asked him one day; I told him I'd met a woman, about the same age as me. She told me her name was Sandra and asked did Matthew ever mention her. Matthew told me she rang a vague bell. I pretended I was jealous – was she a childhood sweetheart? He laughed and said, no, just some mousy kid at school.

She was going to tell Matthew everything that night – I was nothing more than a practice run for her final confession. She knew that Matthew of all people could never live with such a deception and said maybe that's why she likes him.

– But if he does still want me, it'll have to be as Sabina. I'm not Sandra. I never was.

When Sandra left, she left the smell of Sabina behind her, the faint ether of desire. Sandra must be the lie, I thought, not Sabina. It wasn't possible. Then again, neither Matthew or I or anyone else was looking for a Sandra. We wanted a Sabina. Everyone did.

I knew this would shatter Matthew. He would despise her for this. Good. Let him. Let me be Sabina Vasiliev's champion.

I didn't hear from Matthew until Christmas Eve. And then there he was, in my office, pacing up and down again. I stood for Sabina's defence:

– You know she predicted you, Matthew? You are Tomás, the comrade who let her down at the crucial moment. You're deserting her again.

Matthew sneered, said I'd fallen for a stupid girl's fantasy.

– You know your problem, Matthew? For all your political moralism you're still the worst kind of capitalist beancounter or Party aparatchik. You only permit one kind of freedom and it's no freedom at all.

He was a fool. If he'd any imagination or balls he'd be

chasing after her right now. Forget all about Sandra Hamilton, run willingly into the arms of Sabina. If he didn't, then fair game, I would.

But I hadn't counted on the thorough job Sabina had done of covering her traces. On Christmas Day when my family were expecting me home for dinner and while the people of Czechoslovakia were still celebrating their victory, I was wandering the streets near where Matthew had told me he used to kiss her goodnight. The same on Boxing Day, and for days after that. I searched phone books for Hamiltons, rang doorbells. I walked the streets of Glasgow looking for a woman who used to lie naked in a stream in Prague letting the water flow over her naked body. Nothing. Nobody knew her. I began hoping again that Sandra *was* the lie, an elaborate test for Matthew, which he'd failed miserably. Then I met Tereza.

This was months later, when the unsettling colours Sabina had daubed my insides with were just beginning to fade, and I was submitting to my mundane life again. Czechoslovakia was back in the headlines with the news that Havel had officially been made President. It was irksome that Sabina's homeland was now in the realm of general debate and I resented everyone giving their opinions about a country they knew nothing about. They were opening up a secret place and making it susceptible to the creeping ordinariness of anywhere else.

I'd put an ad in the paper for Tereza, stating that I needed to speak to her, and that perhaps I could help her with any legal problems she might have with citizenship, visas, etc. Amazingly, she answered within a week (responding not to the *Glasgow Herald* quarter-page, but to the tiny Classified/Personal in *The List*.) She told me there was nothing she needed done, and claimed that she had no idea of Sabina's whereabouts.

Tereza knew all about her friend posing as a Czech dissident – she had even helped with the details. Apparently they'd laughed about it together, Tereza colluding with the fiction.

– You know you should have rumbled her, she said. – I gave you a clue. Vasiliev's a Russian name.

She hadn't let Sandra use all her story, however. For instance, Tomás had been badly treated in custody, became ill, and died soon after being released. Tereza's father had been arrested after the revolution and was still awaiting trial.

– Sandra, Tereza explained – is a dreamer. Facts like that have no place in dreams.

The two of them could hardly have been more different. Tereza didn't have Sabina's Slavonic looks and brown hair for a start. She spoke more quietly, in more measured tones than Sabina. It was hard to imagine that this small, bespectacled woman had been the real heart of Czech resistance. Sabina fitted the bill more than she did. Tereza was also a practising Catholic, so Sabina must have freewheeled a bit with her version of the love affair in exile with Jurgen.

Tereza lived poorly, in a tiny flat, no money, alone in a foreign place. Although she was hardly the exotic Sabina, she was a connection for me with Sabina's secret country, and I asked her if she'd go out with me. She declined. Although his weakness had let her down badly, Tomás was still her one true love and she was still in mourning for him. Right now she had no need for a man in her life. She smiled and thanked me all the same.

I don't think that much about Tereza or Sabina these days. I miss the Cold War and life now is just as it appears to be. Things between Matthew and me are still a bit strained. I see him around from time to time – he never mentions Sabina, and I'm certainly not going to tell him about Tereza.

He's given up on politics, and I've got back down to work again – the business side of things suffered badly during the Sabina days.

Franny Unparadized

Father McKenna hitched up his vestments, skipped down the altar steps and made such a dash for the sacristy that the boys had to break into a run to keep up with him. An undignified sight, but the good Father had explained to the handful of ladies who made up his congregation that Mrs O'Neil was about to give up her soul to the Lord and needed Father McKenna to supply her with the necessary recommendations and papers.

Before he got to the sacristy door Father McKenna was already pulling off his surplice. Inside, he fired instructions at the boys as he let his vestments drop to the floor reminding Danny of Franny's big sister coming in from work on a Friday night and always closing the bathroom door at the vital moment. He reproached himself for a fleeting image of Father McKenna in bra, pants and tights, when in fact the

Godly man had his black suit on underneath. Father McKenna told the boys to clear up and entrusted to Danny the tabernacle key. He turned to Franny.

'Remember, you. Do as Daniel says. You're here to learn some responsibility. Here's your chance.'

The minute he was gone, Franny rubbed his hands together and ranged around the room, peering in cupboards and corners. When Franny did this in Danny's house and there was nobody in, it meant trouble.

'Just don't, right?'

Franny looked up, offended. 'Just don't right what?'

'Just don't anything. I'm in charge.' Danny jangled the tabernacle keys. Franny's eyes lit up: 'Know what we could do?' Danny felt the kick in his stomach he always felt when Franny came up with an idea. 'Make a host sandwich.'

Danny thought oh shit. This was worse than he'd expected. Trying on the priest's vestments he'd expected. Lighting the candle tapers to make sparklers he'd expected. Taking a swig from the bottle of unconsecrated wine, even. Franny held out his hands for the keys. Danny clutched them tightly.

'It's cool. I did it at that funeral last month when the Dirty Beast was out blessing the stiff. Give us the keys and I'll show you.'

'No way.'

'Suit yourself. I'll use these.' Franny took the cover off the plate that held the hosts.

'Not those! They're consecrated!'

'I know. Holy jam.'

Franny was a mystery. He was wild at the best of times, but with anything to do with the church he was manic. Franny had his own Liturgy, loosely based on the Divine Office. 'Grant Us Peace' = 'Grampa's piece', 'Hail Holy Queen' = 'Hail Holy Queer', 'Go in Peace' = 'Go an' pish', and, at the end of Mass: 'Thanks be to God' = 'Thank God'.

Franny wasn't the craziest guy in school. He couldn't compete with Jazzy and Wetback and Droon-the-Coolies and the rest of them, who jammed the school annexe door shut with an iron bar when all the teachers were still inside then threw blazing torches in through the windows. Franny, being only a 3rd Year, wasn't invited to take part. He was still saveable, so Father McKenna took him into the altar boys to knock some sense into him. It was the best thing that ever happened to Franny. Here he was the toughest, the wildest, peerless. The church was his patch. Here, Franny ruled.

Franny believed in it all. He believed in God. In the one, holy, apostolic Church. He believed in transubstantiation, and he believed that a confession, sincerely and devoutly undertaken absolved him of his sins and assured him a place in heaven. Danny had his doubts, and confided them in Franny, who was genuinely distressed. The ingenuity and sheer force of Franny's arguments comforted Danny and restored his faith.

'What you do is, you take one of these big stormers the priest keeps for hissel, then one of the wee shitey ones that the ordinary smelly folk get, then another biggie. Hey presto – a host sandwich. Wash it down with a chalice of vino. Breakfast of Champions. Brilliant. You try it.'

'No. I mean, I don't really believe it's the body and blood and all that, but –'

'*You* don't believe it? It's got bollocks all to do with whether *you* believe it or not.'

Danny looked on, open-mouthed, as Franny drank deeply again from the chalice.

'Saving grace this stuff. You can taste it.'

Franny was lucky. He could be as wicked as he liked, but still secure in the Knowledge of Salvation. This gave his transgressions a kind of innocence. Franny's badness was upfront, out there, for all to see and judge. But what went on *inside* Danny's mind, his sins of thought, were of a wickedness so black that even Franny would be shocked. There was Franny's sister for a start. And then the involuntary images, like Father McKenna in bra and panties. When Franny got hacked off with a teacher he said so to the teacher's face; he was flung out of class and that was that. But Danny, Danny sat quietly and tortured the offending teacher in hideously violent ways in his mind.

'Well if it's all true, you'll go to hell for that. Those hosts were consecrated.'

'So? So? So I'm bless-ed. Nay, twice bless-ed, cause I had some during the Mass and all.'

Franny swallowed the last of his sandwich. The danger was over. Danny put the hosts and the plate and chalice back into the tabernacle, and locked up.

'I think you've got this all screwed up, Franny. I think you've just invented a wee religion of your own. None of this is exactly what you'd call *normal* Catholicism.'

'*Orthodox* Catholicism, butt-head.'

'Orthodox, well. The priest says the Devil moves in mysterious ways—'

'That's God, ya prat.'

'The Devil as well. He can make it *look* as though it's God talking to you, when in fact it's the Devil.'

'Shite. That's shite. If you do all the right stuff – go to confession and mass and all that keech, big Satan can't touch you. You're protected. It's like your guardian angel's the Terminator. Invincible.'

'See? That's what I mean, Franny. The Terminator was evil. Bent on destruction.'

'Not in Terminator Two.'

Franny had all the angles covered. He had worked it out in detail. Danny, stumped, shook his head sadly, as if Franny were missing the whole point.

'I'll prove it to you. I'll call the Devil up.'

'There's no phone in here.'

'Very funny. I'll call him up. Here and now. Then you'll see who's feart from who. He'll get brown trousers for having been called up in the House of God.'

'Don't be stupid,' Danny said, but he was scared. Franny never failed to deliver once he had come up with a plan. But summoning the Devil was surely beyond even Franny's talents.

'It's pish easy.'

Franny tried to look unconcerned. What if the Dirty Beast comes back?'

'Only takes a jiffy. Don't worry – like I say, when I call him up and he realises where he is, he'll shoot the craw immediately. If he doesn't, I'll waste him.'

Franny's absolute certainty in these matters was breathtaking. He busied himself around the sacristy, whistling softly like he was getting his football gear together or something, while Danny, looked on, stuck fast, at a loss for any argument or action that would stop what was about to happen, happening.

Franny took a candle and placed it in front of the mirror on the huge dressing-table that the priest used for putting on his vestments. He took a bible out of a drawer, placed it next to the candle and rifled through the pages until he found the one he wanted. Then he crossed to the door and switched off the light. The porridge-grey morning was tinted crimson through the stained glass of the sacristy. He lit the candle, which flickered nervously in the half-light, then he turned and explained the procedure calmly to Danny.

'The Devil answers to anything which is the opposite of

God, right? So what you do is, you read the Our Father backwards and look in the mirror. At the end, he'll appear in the mirror. Any questions?'

'Can he come out of the mirror?'

'Usually he would. But not here. He wouldn't dare.'

'Does he appear behind you or in front of you in the mirror?'

Franny considered this for a moment. 'I'm not sure. I think he appears instead of you.'

Danny was alarmed. 'But that would mean you *were* the Devil. It would be your own Devil you'd be seeing.'

'Don't talk wet. The Devil's out there. In Hell. In the Abyss. He comes out and roams the world now and then. It's not like he's inside you.'

Danny looked doubtful. Franny consoled him: 'He appears in front of you in the mirror, then. It just looks like he's taken your place but he hasn't. When he appears I'll stick my hand up in the air and wave to you from behind him. Okay?'

Danny wanted to run. But he couldn't. Something inside of him had frozen his legs. The Devil. The Devil within was waiting so he could expose himself in all his vileness to the body that was Danny and the Evil One's vehicle. Franny set himself in front of the mirror, drew a deep breath, was about to start, then as an afterthought he picked up the priest's alb that was lying on the dresser. He kissed it, mumbled a prayer, put the alb round his neck. He checked the first phrase in the Bible, then stretched out his hands, threw his head back, and in a stern voice, chanted:

'*Amen!* Evil from us deliver . . .'

Danny prayed for the priest to come back. He dreaded his reaction but thought it probably preferable to eternal and immediate damnation. He thought of the fire, the screams of pain, his own included, the tangle of bodies writhing in agony, all of them naked, men and women alike, and amongst them Franny's sister, exposed, moaning in the heat of the flames. The vision excited him, and he knew for sure at that moment that the Devil was not being called up out of the Abyss but out from within his own body. He wanted to warn Franny to turn around, to realise that the danger was not in the glass in front of him, but behind him, inside Danny himself. But he couldn't speak.

'Bread daily our day this us give . . .'

Danny kept his eyes fixed on the mirror, trying not to feel the evil harden and grow in his body. In the flicker of the candle he saw himself walking slowly down a dark corridor, past Mr Donald, the Latin teacher, with his eyes gouged out, screaming with terror. He felt his arm swing through the air and turned to see Wetback clutching his face, blood running through his fingers. He saw himself walk past his own mother and father who stepped aside for him, their eyes averted in fear. And at the end of the corridor, Franny's sister stood in her underclothes and held open the bathroom door for him. He stared hard into the centre of the mirror to see what lay beyond that door.

'Heaven in is it as . . .'

Danny tried to pray. Please God. Oh please please please God. I'll never doubt again. Honest to God I won't. I'll be good now. Don't do this. Please please going not to do this.

He managed to pull his eyes away. He looked at Franny, saw he was clutching, white-knuckled, the edge of the dresser. His voice had slowed, faltered slightly. But he carried on.

'Earth on done be will Thy . . . Come Kingdom Thy . . .'

Franny took deep breaths between his words, but kept faithfully looking up into the mirror at the end of each phrase. Danny managed to snap his eyes shut.

'Name Thy be hallowed . . . Heaven in art who . . .'

Silence. Danny squeezed his eyes shut as tight as he could, the waiting was unbearable. Then Franny's voice lost its gravity: 'You right, Danny, wee man? . . . *Here's Johnny!'*

There was a rush of freezing air. A new Presence in the room. Danny put his hands to his face, and felt tears run through his fingers and down his arm. The Presence in the room hurtled around them, bellowing in some wordless, incomprehensible tongue. Danny sensed the thing move away from him towards Franny. He thought he could hear it leap on him, but Franny's voice squealed out defiantly:

'FATHER OUR!'

Then quiet again. The sound of breathing hung in the air, like frozen breath on a cold night. He heard Franny panting quietly, sucking in air sharply from time to time. Danny wondered where he was. On the ground? Bleeding? Dying? Danny's own breath hummed in his ears, the way it does when you're floating with your ears under the water. He realised he was bent double, on his hunkers, his hands glued to his face. He couldn't move. He'd been like this before: after the Coca Cola ride at the Garden Festival. He'd been so afraid and hung on so tight to the bar in front of him, that when it stopped he could neither get up or let go.

And then there was a breathing, low and deep and angered. It seemed to be working up to an awesome howl. It took voice, rumbling in some deep fury, then broke through and filled the room.

'Jesus Mary and Joseph! What kind of a monster are you!'

It was Father McKenna's voice, but who was he talking to? The Beast? Danny couldn't undo himself to look up. He heard the priest tugging and pulling at something, asking God to forgive Franny of his terrible crime. There was no response from Franny. Just the quiet panting and sucking of air. Father McKenna gave up on him and strode over towards Danny. He seemed a long time coming, and Danny's body curled in a little tighter. He felt the priest right next to him. Danny heard his own sobs echoing through the room. When the priest at last put his hands on him, it was a gentle touch, and his voice was conciliatory. 'Come on now, son. Get up. Tell me what happened here.' He pulled Danny out of his crouch, and took his hands away from his face. Danny kept his eyes closed tight. Behind his eyelids he could see the priest: in bra and panties and tights, his face rouged and lips painted. This was his damnation. This is how he would always see Father McKenna from now on. He would see everyone now bleeding, snarling, naked, writhing in pain and fury.

At last his eyes opened. The room was still flickering red and grey, but Father McKenna was his old self, though his expression was tormented in a way Danny had never seen before. 'Tell me what happened, son.' But Danny couldn't stop sobbing. The priest sat him down, patted his shoulder, then his face clenched like a fist as he turned his attention again to Franny.

Franny stood gawping into the mirror. He was as white as a sheet and oblivious to Father McKenna's accusations and the tugging at his arm.

'You vile, soulless creature. Bad enough spitting in the face of Mother Church, but to terrify the living daylights out of a poor child?'

Still Franny stared at the mirror, his eyes vacant, frightened. Danny managed to get up and go to him.

'Franny? What was it? What did you see?'

'Don't ask him!' the priest commanded. 'If he saw anything it would be the blackness of his own tortured little soul.'

Danny put his arm around his friend's shoulder and asked him quietly again. 'What did you see?'

'Nothing.'

'The mirror . . . ?

'Empty.'

Father McKenna grabbed Franny by the shoulders and pushed him towards the door. 'Get out of here. Don't ever set foot inside this church again.'

Franny shook him off and walked to the door. Then stopped and turned. For the first time ever Danny saw real malice in his friend's eyes. Franny looked at the priest and sneered. 'Don't worry. I'll not be back. What for?'

Father McKenna put his arm round Danny, and they watched as Franny pulled his flimsy jacket around himself and step outside. They heard him mumble as he waded out into the gruel of the evening light: 'There's nothing here'.

Father McKenna spoke softly to Danny. 'Don't worry, Daniel. I know you're innocent.' Danny knew this wasn't true; he knew for certain now that he needed God's and Father McKenna's protection from himself. So he stayed close to the priest and watched his friend scuffing his shoes along the road outside, one more little lost man.

The Soul of Tradition

It's raining again tonight and everything is black and wet except for the people who have covered themselves in colours to keep the blackness out. Mrs McLean shelters in a shop doorway waiting for the rain to let up, ready to make a dash for the bus. Bright anoraks and headscarves and umbrellas flash by like fireflies, but the air is wet and black and seeps into everyone's lungs. A bus flickers dimly up the street and Mrs McLean makes her dash, splashing through puddles and twisting through bodies but the bus doesn't stop and glides by, all lit up and empty like a ghost ship. A wail goes up at the stop and Mrs McLean retreats to her doorway, splashing and twisting again and thinking Friday night and I'm late.

Two and a quarter miles away on the other side of the river La Signora Anarosa Paola di Maio sat up close to the fire, running her fingers through her hair and as it dried fine streaks emerged: silver in dark brown earth. She lifted her cup from the hearth, sipped the tea and examined the room: bare polished floorboards, window shutters, doors, mantel-piece and sideboard all transformed into mahogany out of a tin. Other people thought it was a gloomy room. La Signora thought it cool and shady so that when the window shutters were closed you could imagine you were sheltering from the heat and glare of the midday sun. But they were open now and it was raining and getting dark, and there was still so much to do.

She finished her tea and took the cup through to the kitchen before touring the house for inspection. The hall was clean enough so she left it as it was because she hates it and there's not much you can do with such a pokey wee hall. She went into her daughter's bedroom which was in a real state and began to tidy it up, folding away skirts and blouses and hanging up a coat and a dress, making the bed. The dressing table was a muddle of bottles and sprays, lipsticks, lotions, clasps and little boxes pouring out tangled up neck-laces and earrings and bangles but she left the dressing table alone because she likes it that way. Before she left she set out on the bed her daughter's best underwear, stockings and new dress which she smoothed out with the palm of her hand.

The room next door is her own room, very like her daughter's except that it was neat and tidy. Still she managed to find a few things for the washing bundle, and then opened the wardrobe and selected a dress for herself; put it on the bed and laid the fresh new underwear she'd bought this afternoon beside it. Then it was the bathroom's turn where she got things ready for her daughter's bath, unwrapping a new bar of soap and arranging a little line of shampoo, conditioner, bath salts and talc along the edge of the bath.

She looked at herself in the mirror. In this country you need too many clothes, so she took off her apron and her jumper and then her skirt to see better, stood side on to the mirror, and running her hands first down her back then down her front she seemed pleased enough with the shape she's in, considering her age. La Signora thought of her mother at the same age, skin all dried out by the sun and she reckoned the only good thing about the climate here is at least it doesn't dry out your skin.

In the kitchen there is always a bowl of fresh fruit. Oranges mainly, and on the white walls strings of purple garlic and dried red peppers. The units are all white and the washing machine where she put the bundle of clothes for the wash and the cooker are white and the tablecloth and shelves. Everything white except the fruit and garlic and peppers and the grey window where the rain fell heavily. She checked the wine for tonight's party, the marsala and the brandy. Her daughter would do the cooking when she got in. But she started setting the table, because it was getting dark now and there was still no sign of Rita.

Mrs McLean is standing on a crowded bus which is crossing the river. She has four shopping bags, three of them between her ankles and the other heavier one in her hand. She suspends herself from the rail with her free hand so that she can swing with the motion of the bus, secured at top and bottom. Listening to the rain beat on the tight tin skin of the bus she closes her eyes and slips into a dream. The bus swerves right, then left, in and out of black wet streets. People get off and on unnoticed, the bus careers down hills jogging everybody and then labours back up them again, throwing Mrs McLean around at precarious angles. Rocking about like that she almost falls asleep and nearly misses her stop. She realises just in time, stumbles onto the kerb, shopping bags spinning, and the electric doors snap shut at her heels and the bus roars away behind her. She bends down in the deserted street, finds her brolly and re-arranges her bags, but she can't carry the bags and hold the brolly up at the same time so she gives up and walks to her close, bare headed.

You could really get to hate this city. When it's wet you put on a plastic mac and you end up wetter on the inside. Makes you feel dirty. Some people make you feel dirty. Like McCreavie. But you have to put a good face on it at the office and you end up feeling dirty on the inside too. Nearly home now.

La Signora Anarosa Paola di Maio heard her daughter's footsteps on the stair and opened the door.

– Hi Mama, said Mrs McLean and thought, Friday night, Thank God.

– Hurry dear. We're late.

Coat off, Mrs McLean followed her mother into the kitchen and La Signora took a bottle of wine out of the fridge, showed her daughter the label, who raised her eyebrows and said, ooh nice. She poured out two glasses, they both took a sip and agreed it *was* nice.

– You had your bath yet, Mama?

– Ages ago.

– I'll get the cooking started, then have mine.

The daughter kissed the mother on the cheek and started taking the messages out of the bags, naming everything as she went along: white fish, mussels, prawns, spinach, chicken, olive oil, basil, rice, onions, tomatoes . . . and arranged them all on the work surface until it all looked neat and cheerful and she forgot all about the weather and McCreavie and looked forward to the big evening ahead. When everything was more or less ready Rita went in to have her bath and her mother brought her in another glass of wine. Rita sat up to drink it and let her mother wash her back. La Signora thought her daughter looked beautiful as the water washed away the tired look on her face. Her skin is paler than her own, which is to be expected, and her eyes are serene grey, not brown like hers. She's a little plumper than the Signora was at that age, but that's for the best in a cold place like this. Rita slipped back below the scented bubbles. Her mother said:

– Those boys shouted at me again today.
– What did they say?
– They called me a wop and a stick.
– Spic.
– What?
– Spic, Mama. They called you a wop and a *spic*.

La Signora sipped her wine and said 'I wondered about that.' Then she asked her daughter what a spic is.

– Same as wop. Or maybe it means Spanish.
– Ha! said the Signora, triumphant.
– Or Mexican. Maybe it means Mexican.
– Ha! See? Stupid.
– Unless they *did* call you a stick. That would be more stupid. Or maybe they called you a *mop* and a stick.
– Or a mop *on* a stick' said the mother, and that really made them laugh because La Signora Anarosa Paola di Maio is a cleaning lady. Eventually they stopped laughing and her mother left Rita to finish her bath while she went to continue preparations for the big meal.

A little later, the bath and the preparations completed, the two women went to get dressed in their own rooms. Rita McLean looked out of the window while she tied up her hair. Glasgow in the rain can look like it's dying. The cracks in the paved back court below, which on other days just look like cracks, on wet nights look more sinister, like a cancerous rot that threatens the whole building, the street, the entire city. She imagined that if you kept your eye on them you'd see those cracks running longer, groan open, stretch up the outside walls and curl into her room. She thought of her own house, Mrs McLean's house, which didn't have cracks in the stone or a broken gutter gushing dirty grey water past the windows. Then she thought of Mr McLean and remembered it was his house now. Only the name had stuck. She thought of McCreavie and then her mother and was glad it was Friday and she was home. She shouted through the wall:

– You ready yet, Mama?

– Almost. You?

– Nowhere near.

Next door her mother was spraying on perfume before getting dressed and looking at a photograph lying amongst the make-up and necklaces on the dressing table. There is a man in it, broad and fair with a large moustache and, standing on either side of him, a young girl and a woman who looks not unlike Rita does now, only darker. She picked it up and looked hard at the three of them and especially at the big man with the moustache. Then at the woman who she remembered. Remembered the desire inside her body for the big fair-haired man and the hope she felt when she followed him from a village in the south to a big city in another country. Then she looked at herself naked in the mirror in her room which only shows from her breasts to her knees unless she genuflects a little to see her face. No-one ever sees her naked now, except of course for Rita which is nice in a different way.

– Quick as you can, dear. We'll be late.

Outside the rain is wearing down the long night.

It is midnight now and the big room is empty and the lamps have been turned off, but the fire at the far end of the room still glows brightly. A meal has been eaten, but the table has not been cleared. There are two bottles of wine, one empty, the other almost, dishes piled up on one side, and there are two coffee cups lying next to two brandy glasses. From outside the door a voice calls: 'Rita? Vuoi altro cognac?' From further away Rita laughs. 'Go on then. And put on that record.'

La Signora Anarosa Paola di Maio steps into the room. She is wearing a long black dress of rich organza, trimmed with delicate gold and silver threads. She has gold bracelets on her bare arms, and a gold crucifix lies on the dark skin above her breasts. Long earrings of polished bronze and lace glitter when she moves her head. Her hair is combed and clasped tightly back in matching gold and lace. Her shoes are silken ballet slippers, her lipstick is deep damask, her eyes shaded black with silver dust, her legs, when they appear through the high cut in her dress, bare. When she bows down to take a record from a cabinet by the fireplace, the embers warm the scent of magnolia and she looks very tranquil and very happy. She puts the record on, closes her eyes and waits for the music to start. When it does she moves very faintly, very gently to the rhythm, and softly hums the tune.

Now Mrs McLean joins her, slender in a stark black dress which widens slightly above her black-stockinged knee. She wears no shoes, her shoulders are bare, wisps of cinnamon hair escape from the black ribbon tied behind her head. A cluster of tiny white imitation pearls clings to her long neck, her fingernails and toes are painted lacquer black, her eyes lined with deep black kohl, her lips black too. She reaches across the table for the brandy and pours a little into two glasses. She hands her mother a glass, sits by the fire watching her mother dance, thinking: spic with a mop.

Her mother sings along with the words of the song. What does it say?

– She's asking her lover for her rosary beads back. We

all did that. Gave rosary beads to our boyfriends. We told them they were our mother's but actually we had lots of pairs. She laughs but she remembers that the man with the moustache still had the beads which really were her mother's. She doesn't care. Not really, it's just an old tradition. Still.

The song finishes and another starts, guitars and mandolins in modest familiar rhythm and she turns to her daughter, makes a tiny curtsy and requests:

– Signorina Rita. Vuoi ballare?

Signorina Rita smiles and nods.

– Grazie Signora. I'd be delighted. And coyly, like a teenager at her first ball, she steps forward cautiously and begins to dance.

They dance through the first song and the next song and the next. The mother's steps are bold and confident, the daughter's more tentative, following her lead. The mother keeps her back firmly straight, head thrown back, stretches out her long bare arms inviting her daughter to pass. She does, swirling, the hem of her dress spinning, her eyes glancing in mock coquetry, passing close to her mother, brushing against her dress. Then the mother makes some small stamping movements and with both hands clutches her dress up high above the knee and passes behind her daughter, their two backs touching. Slow, high steps, crossing feet, delicate short steps, turning slowly, then fast, arms kept straight at the side, then lifting, hands moving in soft, slow circles, fingers moving and turning through the air. They dance song after song, dance after dance in front of the crimson dying fire. Their skirts twist and flare and flutter back down, and their shadows breathe against the walls.

They talk in secretive whispers and laugh quietly, as if someone might hear. And all the time that La Signora

Anarosa Paola di Maio and her daughter Rita Francesca di Maio McLean dance and sing happily together the rain hammers relentlessly against the grey window of the big room.

Recorded Delivery

Bloomin' contraption. Now what did she say? To put the tape in you have to press eject. And they think they're so clever these people. Do they not know what eject means? Wouldn't have got though their Eleven Plus in my day. I'd have sent them home with their grammar book.

Look at it. A piece of kidology. Made in Japan. Used to be it was the Americans that made all the fancy gadgets. Hoovers. That was the days when you could name things after Presidents. You'd be hard put to find a President to name something after these days. What could you name after thon wee smug Clinton man? Bare-faced lying. That's what I'd name after him. Bare-faced cheek and fancy women.

Nowadays it's all this Chinese jiggery-pokery. Like the flu. The Bei-jung flu. Oh I had that. You've got to hand it to them – they make a powerful flu. Three months I was laid up for. Just after Kitty and I took the bus down to Helensburgh and we went into that wee restaurant to get out of the rain. Heaven alone knows what the soup was. Soup of the Day was all it was called. Wee white things floating in it. The waitress one of those girls with dreadful diction: 'sux pounds suxty, missus' said they were Nodules. Chinese Nodule Soup. And she was right – there I was two weeks later laid up in bed sweating with the Bei-jung flu.

Play means on.

HIYA AUNT SOPHIE

In the name of God! There's no need to shout.

That's how she always speaks. She thinks I'm deaf. She thinks a lot of things, Farah. *Farah!* Well, I *am* a bit deaf. But shouting doesn't help. Not at all. It's enunciation that's called for. Enunciation. I told all my boys that. Enunciate, and the world's your oyster. Speak properly, and there's nothing can hold you back. They didn't teach that in America. Shouting's the name of the game over there, by all accounts.

And not just loud, mind you. I don't mind the loudness so much. It's the tone of voice. To my mind, there's a way of speaking. Keep your voice nice and sweet. Smile. Even if you're on the telephone, you can *hear* a smile. There wasn't a boy that left my class who didn't go out into the world with good training on how to speak. Lift your voice at the end of a sentence. Change the tone to suit the words. Use *doing* words. That's how to speak. Oh there's some of them that said this lot will only be working on the factory line if they get a job at all. Not the point. *Someone* has to become the managers. And if you've got a good speaking voice, good *delivery*. . . .

Of course, that's all double Dutch to Farah here. A piece of nonsense anyway. Sending a tape. What's wrong with good old pen and ink? At least with your ordinary common or garden letter – not that *they're* that well written, either, I might say – well, you can scan through an ordinary letter can't you? Miss out all the hail-fellow-well-met rubbish. The woman was only over here once. Must be, oh, fifteen years ago now, and she talks like she's known me all her life. She gets that from her mother. Sissy was just the same.

HEY – ISN'T THIS SOMETHING! NOW WE CAN TALK PERSON-TO-PERSON, EVEN WITHOUT A TELEPHONE. I PUT A LETTER IN WITH THE TAPE SO YOU KNOW HOW TO WORK IT – BUT THEN I SUPPOSE YOU MUST HAVE READ THAT IF YOU'VE GOTTEN THIS FAR. WHAT A DOPE! NOW YOU MUST LISTEN RIGHT TO THE END, AUNT SOPHIE. THERE'S A SPECIAL MESSAGE THERE FOR YOU. AND NO FAST FORWARDING – I'VE GOT LOTS OF GOSSIP WHICH I KNOW YOU'RE DYING TO HEAR.

Fast forwarding? That sounds like the ticket for me. How does it work? Must be one of these buttons. Not that one. Easy-peasy Japanesy my foot. That's it.

DID I TELL YOU ABOUT ANGELICA, MY YOUNGEST? MAYBE YOU COULD GIVE HER THE BENEFIT OF YOUR ADVICE. POOR KID, SHE'S HAVING A TERRIBLE TIME AT SCHOOL FAILING ALL HER EXAMS – I RECKON IT'S ALL DOWN TO HER PERIODS. WHAT D'YOU THINK? THE DARLING, SHE'S BLOWING UP LIKE A BALLOON WITH THE CRAMPS EVERY MONTH –

Och in the name of the wee society man! Why can't she just say, Becoming A Lady? That's Farah all over the back. No decorum. And listen to her making excuses for the child. That's what the land of opportunity does for you these days. My boys never had that little miss's chances. But did you ever hear them coming up with bunkum about getting cramps? Not a bit of it.

We'll just have to wind it right through to the end. See what the surprise message is. Bound to be a let-down now.

That's why you should make your main point at the very beginning. In the first paragraph. Everyone knows that. Anyone with a modicum of education. None of this leaving it all to the end nonsense. What *do* they teach them over there?

I've heard it all before, anyway. How Sissy's missing me that much. Pull the other one. Never get a letter from *her*. Not a letter once from Sissy.

Never get a letter from your mother, Miss Farah.

HERE IT IS: TA-TA-RA-RA: THE SPECIAL MESSAGE! BOB AND SISSY ARE THROWING A MEGA-BIG PARTY HERE IN JUNE. IN THE NANTUCKET BUFFALOES AND BEAVERS CLUB. THE SOCIAL EVENT OF THE CENTURY.

Bob and Sissy. Bob and Sissy indeed. Fancy calling your Mother and Father *Bob and Sissy*.

AND GUESS WHO THE GUEST OF HONOUR'S GOING TO BE? THAT'S RIGHT – YOU! SO SORT OUT YOUR GLAD RAGS AND BLOCK OUT A WINDOW IN YOUR BUSY SOCIAL SCHEDULE FOR JUNE. PLEASE COME, AUNT SOPH. MOM SAYS IT'S THE ONLY PRESENT SHE REALLY WANTS FOR HER GOLDEN ANNIVERSARY.

Anniversary? They want *me* to come to their Golden Anniversary. That's a laugh.

Fifty years, though. Hell's teeth. Sissy'll be nigh on seventy. How will I recognise her? She'll be an old woman now. Listen to *me* – I'm one to talk. Just this morning there, Sissy, I was out for my messages. I stopped in front of this shop, to check I had my purse. And I saw the reflection of an old woman behind me in the shop window. I looked round. But there was no-one there, Sissy. Only me. Didn't even recognise myself.

Nantucket. The pearl of the Atlantic. That's what Bob used to call it. One day, we'll go to Nantucket, Soph. That's what he said. Well, maybe fifty years is long enough. And any roads, I won't be going to Torquay this year with Kitty – what with Kitty being dead and all. And I'm sure as fizz not going on my ownio. I always told my boys: there's a time to forgive and forget and you'll know it when it comes.

Fifty years, Sissy. Seems like no time since I saw you off. You looked right bonnie – despite everything. You wore that blue costume of mine, mind Sis? It was that nice, you could have worn it inside out. Unusual shade it was. Blue. Lilac blue. Mind you, I was surprised you could get into it, given the state of affairs. Anyway. Never mind all of that.

WELL, THAT'S ALL FOR NOW. RECORD YOUR MES-SAGE, WITH ALL YOUR NEWS FROM WONDERFUL WON-DERFUL SCOTLAND, POP IT IN AN ENVELOPE AND SEND IT QUICK AS YOU CAN. KISS, KISS. YOUR EVER LOVING NIECE, FARAH.

No tape. You didn't send a tape for the reply, Farah – you big lump. So much for the Oh-such-a-good-girl-that-thinks-of-everything-routine. There used to be some tapes around here. The ones that nice nurse made up with the Bill Jack Show and the Morning Service for Kitty to listen to in the hospital. Where could I have put them . . .?

Here we go. Now what do I press again? Play and Record at the same time. Simultaneously. I suppose I'd better do it the modern way. Leave the acceptance speech to the end. Don't want to seem *too* keen.

'Hullo Farah. Hullo Sissy. Thank you for your lovely letter, Farah. Here I am calling all the way from bonnie Scotland. Everything's fine over here. Weather lovely. . . .

'I was down in Ayr last week. Lovely it was. You'll miss all that, I suppose, Sissy, Girvan and Troon and Barrassie, stuck out there in Nantucket. . . .

'How is everyone with you? How's the family, Farah. . . .?

'How's Robert?'

Robert! Came out without thinking about it. Well it's been Robert, Robert, Robert from Farah for the last fifteen years. I can't go over *there* and start calling him Robert. Not to his face. Start the way you mean to continue, that's what I always told my boys. And the ones that took my advice turned out just fine. Smart, strapping young men that came back to visit me, oh for *years* after I'd left. And those that didn't – well, they turned out just like Robert. Bob. Plenty of money. No moral fibre.

'Here, I was just saying: how will I recognise you, Sis? All I've got's that old picture of you and me and Mum in the room next door. You've got on that black costume. One of those that were all the style at the end of the war. Neat wee American costumes, nipped in at the waist. You've got the white gloves and handbag to go with it. Your "business costume". That's what you used to call it. Business! You worked behind the counter in that grocers' in Royston Road. Dempsey's. The papish place, mind? Oh, Dad was furious with you. Never refused the unopened pay packet, all the same. He thought *I* was wasting my time up at the college. Judging by how I'm dressed in that snap, he might have been right.

'Here, this is a great thing, Sis. Here I am having a cuppa and still talking away quite the thing. As if you were in the room here with me. One lump or two?

'Ach, you were easily the bonniest of the pair of us, Sissy – I don't mind admitting it. Not that I haven't had my share of offers – as well you know. And not so long back either. That lout downstairs, he proposed. Well, I never let him get that far, naturally, but he asked me to accompany him to the dancing.

'As if *I'd* go dancing.

'Mum, God rest her soul, always thought you were the bonniest. Oh, her Sissy could no wrong. Even when you did.

It was Sissy this, Sissy that. As far as she was concerned I didn't know my bahookie from my you-know-what. Her precious Cecilia was always the favourite. No matter that I was the one that stayed here with her and nursed her till her dying breath. No point in complaining about it, Sophie, she'd say. You've only yourself to blame. Sissy's the one that had the get-up-and-go she said. Aye, but not the kind she was thinking about. As if any respectable American employer would have taken on a wee skelf of a lassie with no qualifications to her name and three month pregnant!

'You wait and see Mum used to say. A big healthy man like Bob so far from home, waiting for *you* in America and you go and send your wee sister out to him! By the time you save up the money, Sophie, she said, Sissy'll be a grown woman, and then it'll be too late.

'Well Sissy, I never thought for a moment that she'd be right. Not for a moment did I think that that's how you'd repay me for helping you out. And I *never* thought that Bob – *my* big Bob – would sneak off and marry my own sister behind my back. And you swollen right up with another man's wean!

'Did you ever tell *her* how she started life? Eh? That big eejit of a daughter of yours, Farah – coming over here and writing me letters as if *I'm* the one to be pitied! What a way to bring a daughter into the world. Up a close. Like a dirty wee slut! How could you have, Sissy? Up a close with a man. How could you have even thought about it? Just the very idea – taking your knickers down in a close like that! Were you not worried about infection – opening yourself up like that in a close? Ugh. Even now, the very idea gives me the heebie-jeebies. You manky bitch, Sissy.

'And then you expect me to be all palsy-walsy with the product of your filth.

'And what did you tell my Bob, Sissy? That you were

taken advantage of, I suppose? In the park, maybe? Amongst the bonnie wee daffydillies instead of up a close among the yellow shite?

'My Bob was always the big softy. Over you went giving him your sob stories . . . . and *you* end up being the one walking down the aisle with *my* fiancé – who was supposed to be saving up all his money to buy us a house in Nantucket. No doubt you wore my wee lilac blue suit at your wedding – you could hardly have worn white.

'Oh, but I could have told him, you know. I could have told Bob all about it. Let him know just what kind of a woman it was he was marrying. You didn't think I knew, did you? Oh but I do. I know all the disgusting little details. Kitty told me all about it. How you and her went dancing. About thon yankee soldier you picked up. And Kitty's a fine Christian woman who wouldn't know *how* to tell a lie. She took me there, Sissy. Kitty took me right to the very close.

'It was the most vile place I've ever seen. Made me want to be sick. Men's urine. On the floor and walls, stinking, stinking. A filthy midden. I went in there and I thought of you, standing there, like a whore with your pants at your knees. And I did the same. Oh aye, Sissy. I did. Except I didn't have some horrible American slobbering all over me and poking his drunken thingy into me. Thank God. I just added to the smell, and left.

'I had to tell Mum. I know I promised I wouldn't. But that's before you repaid my kindness of getting you out of Dad's way before he killed you. She'd have found out anyway. The whole close knew about it. The whole street. The whole damned city. And you expected her to forgive you? Our Mum? Forgive something like *that*?

'But I never did say a word to Bob. And I never as much as mentioned it to Farah that time she was across. But what thanks do I get for damning my eternal soul and keeping your dirty little secret from the husband you stole from me? Not a jot. Fifty years, Sissy, fifty years without a word of an apology. And not a penny back for the fare I lent you – or for the wee lilac suit. Sure – plenty of money for big houses in Nantucket and fancy cars and what not – but not a penny for your big sister. Ten guineas that suit cost me.

'Och I know fine what you'll be saying. Can't she just let bygones be bygones after fifty years? This is the first time I've spoken a word to a living soul about what you did to me. Fifty years doesn't seem so long, Sissy. Not long at all. It's no time.'

I mind when we could see nothing but sky out the kitchen window here. Before they threw up those blinking flats. High Living we used to call it. Life On The Top Landing. Now all we get's those families across the way – if you can call them families – running about in their birthday suits half the time. Flats look nice at night all the same, with all the lights on. Like the Queen Mary.

Ach I can't send her that, can I? Hardly the ideal anniversary present for your only sister. Even if she is a deceitful wee besom. Tape-recording's not for me. That's for the youngsters. Let me finish this cup of tea and I'll look out the pen and pad. I told my boys: get to know the rudiments of letter-writing if you want to get on in this world.

Here, there's an idea. You know – I've got just the present for you, Sissy. Hang on till I look it out. That letter to you from Mum.

Och I didn't tell her at all. About you and your shenanigans. I just for a minute there wanted you to think I'd told her. I'd liked to have seen your face. Be like yon Surprise Surprise.

I knew fine she would have forgiven anything you did, her precious Cecilia, and I couldn't have tholed that. She'd never have believed me. She'd have said I was making it all up. *My* Sissy? she'd have said – Never. She'd have called me a pain in the peenie like she always did and ignored the whole thing.

Here it is. She wrote you this letter, Sis. The week before she died. How much she loved you and begging you to come home before she passed away. She gave the letter to me to post. Stamps are forty years old now. Have to put a new one on. Better late than never. I'll just jot a note down on the back of the envelope.

'Give my regards to Bob and Farah. Sorry I can't make the party.'

Eis Wein

I met her a couple of years ago in Spain. We couldn't speak a word to each other and I'm telling you man, it was the best fortnight of my life. Any communication between us had to be purely physical, you know? But seriously, it was like we didn't need words. Like we'd known each other all our lives. We'd walk about all day, and we'd both go to turn the same corner at the same time, or at night, point to the same star at the same time. Like we were soul-mates. Beautiful. Really beautiful. I couldn't speak a word of German and she didn't know any English. We kidded on we were speaking to each other in French, but really neither of us had a scooby what the other one was saying. But in the sack, man, something else. They tell you German's an ugly language. No way, Jurgen. I don't know what she was saying, but that made it all the better. I could translate it in any way

I wanted to. And the things I was saying – Christ, you'd never say it to an English-speaking lassie. Dead dirty and lovey-dovey. She was something else was Astrid.

Then Big Hammy goes and ruins it all. He tried his best all through the holiday, but Astrid and me just ignored him. Snuck off every morning early leaving her gang and my mob slagging us, but we couldn't care less. Hammy had to wait a year to get his own back. I spent eight month at night-school studying German. Got not bad at it. Even got my Higher. See, Astrid was coming to London the next May. She was a waitress in some hotel in the Black Forest and they were putting on some promotion and she was getting a freebie out of it. Hammy and Coco came down with me on the strict understanding that they'd make themselves scarce. Hammy's a seriously damaged individual and Coco can be a right fandancer, but they've been mates all my life.

Of course, Big Hammy turns up at the opening night of the show. I haven't even said hello to Astrid yet, just waved across the room at her. You ought to have seen her in that waitress outfit. I was beginning to think my memory was playing tricks on me, but it wasn't: she was a right ride. Her and the other girls are wandering about the room with trays of snacks and wine. Hammy was getting into one of his moods 'cause they were only giving out pokey wee amounts of each wine. Big Hammy'd been hoping for a major freebie session. Then this German guy starts talking about Eis Wein. Ice wine. Told us they don't pick the grapes till New Year's Eve when they're frozen solid. Stuff costs a bomb. Hammy expresses interest in the design of the label on the bottle. The German guy's pleased and hands the bottle to him for closer inspection. Hammy downs it in a oner. Huns' chins hit the floor. Astrid goes catatonic. She stares at Big Hammy, then over at me.

I let rip at Hammy, loud enough so as Astrid will hear.

Hammy tells me to fuck off. Later, Astrid and I get talking. We'd never *talked* before, mind? But now I'm gassing away like a good one, dead proud of my German. And that's when I find out she talks a load of pish. First about Hammy, which she goes on and on about. But then about everything else, too. Now that I can actually talk to her, I realise she's a moron. I mean, I'd still have screwed her, but she's not the pure soul creature I'd thought she was. Also, it's pretty clear she's none too impressed with the new talkie version of me either.

So that was that. No more Astrid, and Hammy hasn't spoken to me since. So I'm stuck with Coco, who, like I said, is a fandancer.

Another City

I am the Water Lady. They tell me in here that some time in the future, I'll be a tourist attraction. Little expeditions will be organised around my old haunts. Not that I'm the only murderer, or even murderess around these parts. At one point there were twelve of us with cases in progress; two of the defendants women, and one of those being, like me, accused of murdering her husband. But only my case made the headlines.

Already a small body of literature has grown around the various theories of how I killed my husband: I waited until he was drunk, dragged him to the bath, held his head under the water, dragged him back out; I waited until he was asleep, or knocked him out with a heavy object, then poured a measuring jug of water, either down his throat if his mouth was open, or into his nostrils if not. Neither of these is likely

(I was about to say, holds water). My husband enjoyed a drink, fairly regularly after that first argument between us. But he never drank to the point of losing consciousness. He was a light sleeper. He was a large man, heavy, and I am not strong. At the time of the alleged crime, it was plain to see that I was very weak indeed, even by my standards.

But it is the presence of the salt in the water that drowned the deceased, which has caused the most debate. The most absurd explanation has it that I urinated into his open sleeping mouth, only later filling him up with tap water. Apparently the coroner's report couldn't rule this out, and a medical examination proved that I do consume a lot of salt. But it does not explain the traces of other substances generally found only in deep sea water. Even this was easily explained away: I collected the sea water previously, adding it later to the tap or bath water which eventually filled my husband's lungs. A red herring. But the urination idea caught the public imagination: it was suggested that I drank the sea water, before peeing it down my victim's throat.

His body was found on the bedroom floor. There was a small pool of water round him, hardly enough to drown a man. Initially the police thought he had died from a blow to the head, judging by the nasty bruise he had sustained above his left eye. Later, once the coroner had reported death by asphyxiation, they decided the bruising must have been a result of his fall, or received earlier during a struggle between us. There was a knife lying by his side. A Sabatier vegetable knife, smeared with human blood. But the blood did not belong to either my husband or I, but to another, unidentified person. I could not help them clear up whose it might have been. The mysterious blood gave rise to suspicions of other atrocities perpetrated by me, but no evidence has yet come to light. The handle of the knife gave no clues, it looked as though it had been washed – possibly in sea water again.

Neighbours – people with whom we rarely associated and therefore knew little of our lives – reported raised voices on the night of the killing. A male voice, screaming, frightened. And a female voice, shouting loudly, as though urging someone on. Some of the neighbours thought there may well have been a second male voice.

My lawyer urged me to plead guilty on grounds of diminished responsibility, which I did, although I am not at all sure that I was the murderer. Maybe there were times I wanted my husband dead. Or perhaps not dead; disarmed. Neutralised. We often desire the destruction of our guardians. I was instructed to pledge that I had no memory of what happened that night, which, by and large, is true. The fact is, by the night of the killing I was already unable to separate one day from the next. I have a memory of being in the house, and then, later, going out into the garden. But these are recurrent activities, and could be memories of any evening. I only remember the police arriving in my bedroom. I remember because it took me a moment or two to realise that I was naked, and surrounded by uniformed men, staring angrily at me. If it is possible to have a memory of something which did not happen, then I have to say I can only remember *not* murdering my husband.

I am allowed to receive and read the papers here. The local press have made a great fuss of the case. It is, after all, something of a bonanza for them. The reports are good-humoured in the main. Murder between consenting adults. Quiet and respected businessman drowned by his mature but elegant wife (their words, not mine). A wife who, they imply, it is not impossible to imagine having an affair. And, being generally considered courteous but taciturn, a bit of a dark horse, it is equally not impossible to think her capable of drastic action, should any such affair have come to light.

I read my papers by the window, high up in this building

which towers over a part of the city I do not know. The streets out there are angular, like arrows, spiking one another. It occurs to me now what a miracle it is that any of us manage to find our way about. So many crossings and corners. From my vantage point up here, the city resembles a scattering of crucifixes. The days here are samey. They go from dawn to dusk to dawn again. It never gets bright, and it never gets properly dark. Pale dawn to dull dusk.

There's another city. It lies flat in the water like a golden coin, a reflection of the moon. It's perfectly round, and all its streets are circular, leading back to their starting points. I come here a lot at night. I like the circular streets. It's impossible to get lost, even in the darkness which sometimes gets so black it hurts your eyes, like a glare. Keep walking in any direction and you'll eventually get to where you're heading for. You can slip from one street into another via little curved alleyways.

For years I walked round the city alone. Wandering through the darkness, enjoying the coolness of it against my skin, oblivious to the locals who passed me by. I basked in the thickness of the night, closing my eyes against it as if against a dark sun.

They have days here, too. They must have. But I've never felt tempted to come then. It's like when I was young and my parents took me every year to the seaside. It was a magical place, that. Every year we'd go to the beach, and the fair with its lights and tinny music. We used to go out on the water, the three of us, on a little boat. Or sometimes just my Mum and me, bobbing along on the water, my head on her lap. The sea always twinkled, full of tiny submerged stars. I used to think that place was newly created for me every year, that it and all its people stopped existing from one holiday to the next. Then one year, after Mum's death, Dad took me in wintertime. I didn't want to go. Not then, not without mum. But he said he'd promised her, and that we had to. I saw my beautiful village for what it was then. Just another dreary town, half-empty, the wind rattling the closed signs, and the sea dull and cross. That's why I don't want to see my city in any other way than the way I first found it: dark.

There's a kind of safety in the night here. There're no shadows. In the doorways and alleys the dark only glows brighter, like jet. Of course, the city is like any other, it'll have its dangers; but they can't hide from you. There's nowhere for them to jump out from and surprise you. And the circularity of the streets: that makes you feel safe, too. I've heard newcomers say it confuses them – it never confused me. Admittedly, the streets look quite alike, but you can distinguish them easily by the depth of their curve: shallow, almost straight, near the rim; tight near the centre.

The centre is a square – an oval, really – where they sell flowers round the fountain. Every so often they hold a celebration here, and wine (imported presumably – there are no fields in the city, surrounded completely by water) is piped through the fountain. In a hundred years, not one drop has ever touched the ground. Bottles, cupped hands and open lips joyfully gulp it up out of the air. It was at one of these celebrations that I first met my friend.

She's a little older than me, and not a visitor, but a native of the city. She's very beautiful, which is both what drew me to her and made me keep my distance for so long. She has long thick hair, reddish, depending on the quality of the darkness. The skin on her face is lightly marked, the result of some childhood illness, a pattern of tiny burrows and dimples in which the darkness moves, giving a new tint and sheen to every expression. Her smile is miraculous; it etches out her eyes, the folds of her skin, the kindness of her mouth.

Together, my friend and I go walking in the late evening, arm in arm, taking the longest route round to the city centre, where we sit and look at the flowers. The piercing colours of them against the black night: green, red and the most finely tuned whites, their perfumes sailing and swirling. I'm happy here, in the pillowy dark, in the streets that wrap around you like an embrace, with my friend, her shadowy smile rippling.

I once told my husband about the other place. The doctor

who comes to visit me here thinks that might have been when our troubles began. But that's not true. They began long before that. When we were courting we had an unsettled relationship. People find this hard to imagine. Anyone who knew my husband thought him a calm and genial man. Centred. Decisive. That was how he appeared in business. His success was based on his ability to, in his words, roll with the punches. He took adversity in his stride, and tackled new challenges positively, thus rising swiftly up the promotion ladder. It was important to him, to us, to our continued advancement, that this is how the world should see him. And quite rightly so. It is a vicious world, and our opponents would seize on any opportunity, any glimmer of weakness, to do us down. My husband always appreciated my role in our partnership. I, too, worked, and he supported me in that. My business – a small retailer of quality, mainly Italian, kitchenware – was a client of his company. I knew as much about income and expenditure, resource management, accounts analysis, diminishing capital value as he did. His colleagues used to say how much they wished their wives were as fluent in the language of commerce as me. We were a proper partnership.

We supported each other in more personal ways, too. I, the vessel to contain the failures, the setbacks, the horror he experienced every day of his working life, but concealed from his colleagues; he, the stalwart against my fear of flickering out. Since an early age, I have lived with the feeling that my life is dimming. Or rather, that the world is dimming around me. There were days when I walked to work and could not feel the ground under my feet; when I held conversations but could not hear the voices, not even my own. This tendency gave others no cause for concern – I was merely dubbed as being a little vague. An attractive quality in a woman, they said. Eventually however, the encroaching absence had a detrimental effect on my business. At the time of the alleged murder we were still in profit, but only just.

The other woman who was being tried for the murder of her husband at the same time as me had the mitigating circumstances of domestic cruelty in her favour. My husband had never laid a finger on me. Only once, during a particularly painful time for him, and not long after the child we had fostered was returned to its mother, did he threaten me. For years, I had been going out for long evening walks, or sitting in the garden, or simply looking out our bedroom window into the alder trees that lined the streets, their tiny round leaves trembling, with excitement or fear I could never decide. I found these periods of quiet refreshing and my husband initially encouraged them. By the day he threatened me, however, he had begun to see my temporary absences as a kind of desertion, not just of him, but of our partnership.

The change in his attitude came, I think, when I began to return from my walks, or periods alone, tired and sleepy. At first I had returned invigorated, ready to talk through the problems of our respective days, and eager to have sex. But, increasingly, my expeditions left me slumbery, slackened. It took a while for this change to have an effect on my husband. My capacity for listening had improved: I felt less need to talk about my day, or to offer unnecessary advice on his. I felt I could serve him better by hearing him out, let him siphon off the frustration and the bile that had gathered in him since morning. And we continued to make love regularly. I became more passive, yes, but like a drunken woman, limp, unscandalized, perhaps a little lascivious, happy to let him move around me, to clutch and knead my flesh. If anything, I became more attracted to his angularity, his rough edges. His elbows, knees, penis which had once appeared potentially damaging, now looked smoother, more ductile; my body would not be bruised by them, but would revive around them at their touch.

He saw it differently. I was drawing away from him, from our domestic and business partnership. He felt a failure on his own part, a failure to keep me firmly on track, feet on the ground. He was not a violent man, not like those you hear of, sporty types who feel their bodies to be more than merely the container of their selves, aggressive men who fist-beat tables in arguments. He was not like the husband of the woman accused, and convicted of murder just before I was. I knew my husband was not going to harm me. Not that night. Though for the first time since I'd known him, I saw it possible, faintly possible, that he may sometime in the future. At that moment, however, his anger was a wave that had already broken, I was merely being stung by the spume. That is why I handed him the knife: to make it absolutely clear to him, to us both, that this outburst would not, could not, turn itself into action. He took it from me, and cried. Slumped in his chair, he let the knife drop to the floor beside him, and wept, wept so very sadly, asking me to forgive him.

But it worked, this warning. For a while after I felt less absent, did not allow myself to retreat so much. I asked him to be ever vigilant over me; to be my anchor against slipping away again, and he promised he would. He promised he would be strong for me.

It was my friend's suggestion. She said we couldn't spend the rest of our lives walking round and round the evening streets, and sitting among the flowers when we arrived at the centre of the city. We changed our itinerary, meeting first by the fountain where we waited for each other seated on the carpet of petals, then headed outwards, twisting round the unwinding streets towards the rumble of the sea in the distance. The walk, provided we didn't take too many diversions down alleys and doubling back on ourselves, took an hour or so. There were many things to look at: the carvings on the wooden buildings, gargoyles for the most part, but sometimes shipsheads, pinned to walls, in the shape of birds, or sirens, mermaids, stars. My friend lived closer to the sea than to the centre, precisely where I don't know. She sometimes stopped and talked to people who were heading in the opposite direction. Neighbours, I imagine, but I could never catch their conversation for the loudness of the sea in this district. When we arrived at the rim, we would sit on the rocks.

The city is held out up from the water by huge stone cubes, large enough to lie out on without reaching the corners with your outstretched legs and arms. At their highest point, closest to the most outwardly street, the cubes are piled four high. Below, the ocean gnaws away at the lowermost rocks, whittling them down from cubes to horseshoe shapes and semi-circles. It was while we were sitting on one of the high stones that she yelled to me over the din of the tide. I saw her lips move, the shadows dancing on her face, but it took the sea-wind a moment to carry her words to me. Someone she wanted me to meet. Her son.

I thought I'd heard wrong. It'd never occurred to me that she had family of any kind. She never mentioned father, mother, sister or brother to me in all the time we spent walking together. Least of all had I imagined she had a husband, let alone a son. I still don't know if she has a husband – I get the feeling I shouldn't ask. I've never been to her house, so I don't know who lives there with her. Her son lives by himself.

That night, after we had walked far enough away from the sea to be able to speak again without shouting, she told me it'd be good for both her son and I to meet. She arranged to take me to him the following night. I couldn't see why not.

The improvement in our domestic life did not last long. His life outside the house was on an even keel, ironically thanks to the recession: the pressure was off him a little as no-one's expectations were high, and his position was secure enough within the hierarchy. The economic climate meant the slight upturn in my business affairs after our argument was to be short-lived. My husband never lost his temper again. But we were both weakening: my absences became longer, more regular, and his attempts to curtail them had little effect. He had taken to coming in at night and sitting silently in his chair. There was little to talk about anyway. It was as if our lives outside the house had been petrified, and the spell had seeped in past the draught excluders and the proofing round the windows into our home. The most he could do was let his hand dangle over the arm of his chair, his fingertips above the knife which he had dropped there and which had never been removed. A sign that he was still vigilant.

When I was a girl, I spent some weekends with an aunt and uncle. They never spoke to one another. They weren't angry with each other; on the contrary, they were very tender. They touched a lot. They'd just lived so long together there seemed to be nothing they needed to say. They spoke to me, of course. On the Friday evenings when I arrived, they would babble endlessly, letting out all the words they had had no use for since my last visit. They'd both speak about the same things, things they had observed together. But they spoke about them at different times, so that their conversation overlapped in strange ways, and I would come home and tell my mother hybrid stories, and she'd laugh and tell me that that couldn't possibly have happened. One night, while I was staying over at my uncle and aunt's, I couldn't sleep. I went downstairs to get a cup of water – their house was always like a furnace. As I passed their open bedroom door, I heard voices. I looked inside. They were facing away from each other, their rumps touching in a heap at the centre of the bed, and they were sound asleep. But they were having a conversation. I stood there listening to them talking, exchanging little inconsequential but, I now realise, necessary details of life. Who would go to the shops tomorrow; what they would buy. They asked one another how they were feeling, and talked of their aches and pains. I realised this was the only time they ever spoke to each other. I listened to them assure each other everything was fine, especially now that I was here, and then I watched as they fell back into silence.

I told my friend this on the night she took me to see her son, and she seemed to understand something about the story that I did not. I told her because, when we went there, her son was asleep. He lay in a long, narrow bed, in a brown wooden room, while the night shone outside his window. I could not believe he was her son. He was a man, I'd say in his late twenties. I didn't think my friend was so much older than me. She must have had him when she was very young. She asked me to sit with him, and told me he doesn't wake up very often. When he does he has to go quickly to the boats, and go out and fish in the ocean. When he returns he's exhausted and sleeps again. He likes company, however, when he's asleep, and my friend told me he had expressly asked for me to come and sit with him. He had seen me from his window when she and I had been out walking. I was surprised, and I admit, a little flattered. But when I tried to find out more, or why my friend thought it would be good for me to sit with him, she merely said he had wanted it that way, and if I did, too, then that would answer all my questions.

Night after night I came back to that little wooden room, and sat by this sleeping man, on a chair his mother had left for me. For a long time he never woke up, but I got the impression he knew I was there. I spent the hours either looking out the window, or at him. He wasn't handsome. Not in the way my husband was. He was coarser featured. Not stronger, not more manly. Thinner; he had the same marks on his face and body as my friend, little dents and hollows in his skin where the darkness gathered in tiny, ebony pools. After a while I got the courage up to dip my finger into those pools, on his chest, his cheeks, his arms. He would stir lightly, but not waken.

Then one night he did. He opened his eyes and smiled at me, and stood up without yawning or stretching. He went to his window and looked out. He wasn't parading his nakedness. He knew I had seen him from every angle while he slept. It was pleasant to see him move his body, though, the shadows flowing over him like the reflection of a dark stream. He came back from the window and sat on the bed in front of me, his shoulders towards me, legs open. This was how I sat, watching him, when he was asleep. Sometimes naked, too. I'd taken to wearing a light tunic during the warm nights, and in this room where the darkness couldn't circulate, it often got warm enough for me to take it off. He stretched his arm under the bed and pulled out his clothes. Waterproofs and boots. He put them on, smiled at me and left.

In nearly ten years there was only one important change. I can't say precisely when it happened. All I can remember is that for a long time the knife lay in the corner on the floor where he had dropped it by his chair, and then it was in his hand. He would come in every night, sit in his chair, pick the knife out of the magazine pocket in the arm, and hold it, its blade pointing outwards into the kitchen. Previously, he had helped out a bit with the cooking, but now he sat and waited until I served it to him. He ate it with one hand, never letting the knife drop from the other. At the end of the evening he would take it upstairs with him, place it in the pocket of his pyjama jacket until he had changed, then hold it again as he got into bed. Before falling asleep, he placed it on the bedside table, picking it up again in the morning, reversing the process, and carry the knife back downstairs to his chair where he had his breakfast.

Why did I not remove it – either from the chair while he was out, or from the bedside table when he was asleep? I do not know. I reasoned that he could easily get a replacement knife. I told myself that, as it was I who had given him the knife in the first place, I could not now confiscate it. Of course I knew that the mere act of taking it away from him would be an important gesture. Perhaps it would even break the habit. But it seemed too great a risk. Taking away his protection – which both he and I pretended was *my* protection, protection from myself, from my desire to slip away from obligations and liabilities – taking it away from him, I feared would cause a terrible upset. I could not imagine what the outcome of such an upset might be. Until then, my husband had been the rock in the social world to which I had moored myself. Now it was he who wandered in a private world, the dimensions, colours, nature of which were a frightening mystery to me.

I could have left him, and I thought about it. But leaving was precisely my problem. The very thing I had to do less of.

One evening my friend came round to the wooden room unexpectedly, and found me lying naked on the bed next to her son. I leapt off the bed, pulling my tunic on, apologising ashamedly for my behaviour. She didn't seem to notice either my apologies, nor anything strange in the position she'd found me in.

That was the night she told me the story of the stars. Some ancient Goddess, Juno I think, nursed a dying man in the heavens, supposedly above this city. He was getting very weak the man, and Juno nourished him by offering him her breast. The man fell asleep, and his head rolled from her breast onto her shoulder. Juno's milk spilled from her breast, dropping into the night sky, filling it with stars. The stars you can see out this window here, my friend said, are Juno's light embrace.

Then she said something that surprised me. She said, why didn't I bring my husband with me next time I came to the city? I didn't realise I had ever spoken about my other life – that life in the place that goes from dawn to dusk to dawn again without ever getting properly dark. I was sure I never mentioned my husband. And anyway, how could I possibly bring him here?

The worst of it was no-one outside the house noticed any change. He was still the same gentle, pleasant man he had always been. If anything, his working life had become easier. Despite the continuing decline in his company's performance, he was promoted. He was no longer anxious about his career or his standing in the world. He adapted well to this new domestic life of ours. We stopped socialising, an activity he had always been assiduous in maintaining on a regular basis. He lost interest in how my shop was doing. He was content. Content, for the first time in his life. Content to sit there, in his armchair, with his knife, and wait for the following day to begin. He was not actively unpleasant to me. It was as if he was not there at all: just his body, his hand and the knife.

I spoke to him about it one evening. He agreed that he felt calmer than he had ever done, but that he did not think it could last forever. I was not to think that because he had never used the knife that he would not, at the right time. When that time would be, he said – and I believed him – he did not know.

Now I could not move forward or back. Forward lead into the knife, which he pointed at me from his chair, its blade following me round the room. (Even when I left the kitchen, I could feel it through walls, homing in on me, finding my precise position, its steel chilling my skin.) Backwards meant slipping forever into the dark, my life bleached out of the world, the fate I had struggled against for so long. It was to halt my retreat that I was now being held at knife-point.

It was about a year ago now when, despairing, I told my husband what went through my mind when I was alone in the garden, or out walking. He found it distasteful. He did not become aggravated. Did not shout or rage. He merely looked at the knife, its blade dull now, sweat and finger stained with so many years of handling, and told me that I had become a stranger to him. Perhaps I had always been a stranger. But how much easier it would be to spear the flesh of a stranger: none of the responsibility of hurting a loved one, none of the remorse. Simply insert the knife and be done with it.

Of course I couldn't bring him with me. The idea's absurd. I told my friend and she shrugged. I told her son, my man-friend, as we stood by the window one night, while he was getting ready to go. I watched him slip on his waterproof clothing, its cold oily skin disconnecting me from the soft shadows of his body, his downy hair, the dark pearl of his sex, so that now I was the naked one, and the breeze from the sea behind me made me shiver. As he left he told me that, one day, this man of mine that I wouldn't bring with me, would come of his own accord.

He began following me around, physically, holding the knife blade an inch or two from my skin. He reminded me that I had made him promise to protect me from myself. He could no longer trust me to be alone. He phoned his office and told them he was taking some of the holidays he had never claimed in ten years. He was now in such a position in the company that no-one would dare refuse his request. His colleagues were delighted: he needed a holiday. They told him to take as much time as he needed, spend a little time at home, do nothing in particular, just relax with his wife. He instructed me to tell my staff that they would have to get on without me for a few weeks.

He never left my side. He stood by me while I prepared the food, escorted me to the bathroom, followed me out into the garden when we needed to dispose the rubbish. We had to go to the supermarket once, and he held the knife in his jacket pocket while we shopped, nodding to neighbours and acquaintances. He got up when I did, retired when I did. And we slept fitfully, closer than we had for many years, though I faced away from him, feeling the knife pressed against the small of my back.

On the night he died, I had managed to sleep. I was very

tired, and although I could hear my husband shouting, I could not wake. I tried to, I think, but my sleep that night was like a wall, a huge high wall of solid rocks. I tried to clamber up them, hearing his shouting, even though I sensed that danger lay at the top. But anyway, it was impossible: the surface of the rocks was smooth and hard and without footholds and I slithered back down into sleep.

I awoke when my man-friend leapt out of bed and ran to the window. I opened my eyes and saw his mother sitting beside the bed. She must have been watching over us while we slept. They said something in urgent voices to each other, but I wasn't properly awake and couldn't make out what was up. He quickly pulled on his waterproofs and ran to the door. My friend handed me my tunic, I put it on, and followed them out of the room into the night. We ran in single file – my man-friend first, then his mother, then me – up the half-moon alley and onto the street, following the curve round towards the sea. We were heading for the south shore of the island, where the sea is roughest. We weren't kitted out for the weather here, where the sea-spray stings like daggers and the waves bark furiously.

Like the time my father took me to the little sea-side town for the last time. We waited all week for the rain to stop, before taking the boat out, the way we used to. On the last day, it pelted down worse than ever, but he insisted on going. This was his last chance. He told me to stay indoors, but I followed him down to the boat house, getting soaked. I wanted to stop him but I knew I couldn't. He struggled like a madman to get the little rowing boat out onto the water, the waves throwing it back at him. He screamed and yelled at it, like it was a pet dog that had gone crazy on him. At last he succeeded in getting it out onto the water, and then scrambled inside. I watched as he ploughed the boat through thick, black gluey waves. I think I was shouting at him to come back, but can't be sure: that was the first time I couldn't hear my own voice. He managed to get himself quite far out, so that he became very small in the distance. But I saw him stop, stand up in the lurching sea and empty my mother's ashes into the waves as he had promised. He made it back to the boathouse alive, but suffering from a kind of deathly exhaustion he never recovered from. He had left the urn that had contained my mother's ashes in the boat. I picked it up and carried it home, struggling with the weight of the heavy sea-water.

By the time we reached the tumbling stone blocks that veil the city from the sea, my man-friend had disappeared from sight. His mother and I clambered over the high rocks and started making our way down through the clefts between the rocks. Halfway down we came across his waterproofs. We looked out to sea, and saw him battling against the snarling waves, their white teeth snapping at him. Further out, just visible in the dark, was another man, screaming for his life. My man-friend made it out to him, put his hand out for the stranger to catch hold. Instead of doing so, the drowning man pulled his arm up out of the water, and started to slash out wildly at his saviour with a knife. The young man was hurt – we could see him clutch his shoulder. He grappled with the stranger, trying to pull the knife off him, the two of them vanishing every now and then below the sea's surface. When the wind swirled round in our direction it carried their voices to us, spluttering and wailing. I couldn't hear my own voice, the wind sucking it from my lungs and throwing out into the night. And I couldn't hear my friend's voice either, though she was standing right next to me, screaming out at her son. By the look on her face, and by the blackness of the shadows that danced on it, I think she was shouting at him to leave the murderous stranger to die.

I genuinely did not remember at the trial. If I had remembered, I would have said. Perhaps I'll tell the doctor today. I think it was that night, the night my husband died, I'm sure it was, I came across an old metal jar, a vessel or urn or something, at the back of the bedroom cupboard. Was this while I was still half-asleep? I know that in the days before my husband died I had taken to cleaning out the house, as if getting ready for some move, some future closing-up of the family home. I remember the jar was heavy, full of liquid. I carried it (before my husband started screaming in his sleep, or during, or after?) carried it out of the room. I cannot remember where I took it, but only that I was tired from the effort when I returned.

We made our way back slowly to the city, my friend and I, not saying a word to each other. We walked up the spiral wooden stairs to the room where her son lived, and sat on either side of the bed. Without saying a word, she took out from under the bed the urn which had held my mum's ashes. Then, smiling at me, she took it under her arm, and left the room. I watched her walk away. She looked so very sad, but still as strong and bold as ever, the shadows rippling across her body. I lay down on the bed.

It was darker that night than I'd ever seen it, even here. I knew morning must be on its way and I really should go. But I lay on, across the bed. I couldn't see my own body, not even the outlines of it. I stretched my arms and legs out over the sides of the bed, so that none of my surfaces met. Without sight or touch, I felt I was floating, cushioned on my own heartbeat, alive to every particle of my body, every follicle. I listened to the slow, deliberate churn of my stomach and bowels, to my breath pumping through me from head to foot, my blood streaming, down endless tiny alleys that mapped out the form and shape of me, melting into the darkness. It felt like my body was flowing outwards, breaching its own edges, spilling out, becoming rounder, seeping across the room.

That was how the police found me. Lying naked on top of the bed, my husband dead on the floor in a pool of water.

The lady who comes to see me in here is very kind. She brings me cards and letters from well-wishers, all opened, but sometimes some of the hate-mail slips through. I pretend not to notice and don't mention to her. She tells me I won't be here for long, reports to me about Courts of Appeal and petitions and lack of evidence. She tells me to 'hang on in there'; I'll be out of here in no time.

I've not been back since. I know I should. See how he is, make sure he wasn't hurt by the drowning stranger. Or worse. If it were really bad, I'm sure my friend would contact me. I think one day she might come and see me here. That'd be nice.

A colleague from work, unfortunately without a job now since my shop closed down, brought me my veil. It was good of her. It's a dark blue veil I wore at my wedding (I was not a virgin bride). My mother gave it to me a long time before, when I was a child. She used to put it on my head so that it covered my face and the two of us would laugh. I liked the way the world looked through it: soft and blue, my mother kneeling down and smiling through it at me, her face mild like an angel's. It's got darker with age, the veil. When I hold it up now to this window that looks out over the crosses and spikes of my home city, it makes the place look much darker. It makes it look as though night has come, at last.

A Scottish Soldier

Another day in bed. GEORGE has got lost in the tunnels that honeycomb SMUGGLER'S TOP. In this room the electric light has yellowed out the day and the gas fire mutters on. From time to time big Geo and Alec take a break from PENALTIES in the back court to shout up at the room, but I'm too sweaty and haven't the energy to go to the window to defend myself. This is the third day now, and we've settled into a regime. Breakfast in bed: tea, toast and four doses of strawberry flavoured Ephedrine with a plastic 5 ml spoon and instructions to take each dose half an hour before dinner, tea and supper. Means no-one has to come traipsing to and fro from the room like a yo-yo. Someone's been given the job of exchanging the library book every morning, and they leave it deliberately late till just before lunch so that I'm not moaning about being bored before supper. I'm allowed up for the ONE O'CLOCK GANG, but not for the WHITE HEATHER CLUB, which is on tonight. Geo and Alec have moved on to BEST MAN FALL. Someone brings in my tea, two plates sandwiched together with gammon and turnip and potato trapped inside. A glass of water and a bright purple pill whose name I can't remember. I bury the turnip into the potato with the distant thud and clap of Geo and Alec's war in the back court. I save the Ephedrine up for pudding. It's all gone quiet outside. Then Alec asks Geo what way is he supposed to be dying now and Big Geo shouts up for my benefit: VERY VERY SLOWLY LIKE BERNIE. I tell him having asthma isn't dying ya prick but I don't shout it out, so nobody hears me.

Tonight's the night for the WHITE HEATHER CLUB. The house becomes the way my mother says it used to be in her day, full of people singing but with the telly in the middle now instead of granddad with his fiddle. Aunts and uncles and people who call themselves aunts and uncles and neighbours who don't have a TV or just fancy a singalong, get together in our kitchen. The whisky gets taken out. I'm not allowed up for it, even when I'm not sick. I can hear it though, even now. HEATHER CLUB night is also the night I'm likely to get my visit, depending on how well ANDY STEWART has set the mood. Which is why I still remember it now.

On my bed there's a trumpet, SMUGGLERS TOP bent back at the first page of the last chapter, and a plastic steering wheel with gear stick which everyone thinks it's ridiculous to be playing with at my age, but travel is freedom after all. I've driven to the YUKON which is my favourite place, cause it's cold and crisp and gives you goosepimply shivers the way clean sheets do. The sheets aren't clean just now, they're limp and wet which is just as well, and roasting on the side nearest the fire. I have to make intermittent noises on the trumpet so that no-one complains I'm not practising.

Mr Lutovsky is due tomorrow. The visit is always the night before the trumpet lesson. I used to hope that that would make my arpeggios better, a little experience of real life. Mr Lutovsky's a man of experience. He's from Poland and was a count or a duke or something and stinking rich before he had to run from the NAZIS or the COMMIES or someone. When I'm sick Mr Lutovsky sits on my bed and I play in my pyjamas while he watches me with sad eyes. He'd said I'd never be a musician, which I must admit put me off him a bit, but that I'd always love good music, and that was more important. The old dears didn't like the sound of that one bit, and I knew that this would be the last lesson, which it was.

I usually save the last chapter for after supper. I'm tempted to read it now, because tonight, what with the HEATHER CLUB and then the visit, there will be less time to kill, and usually I don't feel like reading after the visit anyway. I don't really like the FAMOUS FIVE all that much and everyone knows that but whoever's been given the library run doesn't care. They're like a dull thump, JULIAN and TIMMY and the rest, though GEORGE interests me. They make you feel fed-up while you're still reading them. I like THE CALL OF THE WILD and WHITE FANG and all that stuff which only makes you feel fed-up when you finish it. I pick the book up anyway and let the secrets of SMUG-GLERS TOP blunt the worry of waiting.

They're trooping into the hall, the HEATHER CLUBBERS. The door's been left open for them, but they shout into the kitchen to make sure it's all right and someone shouts back and tells them to come on in it's just starting. I listen out for the visitor's voice, though I know he's as quiet as a lamb. That's the thing about the visit, if you knew for certain it was going to happen you wouldn't want it to. It's not knowing and wondering if the boredom's going to be broken tonight that makes it interesting. Big Geo and Alec are out in the back again after tea, someone's coaching them in the finer points of ball control. It could be the visitor but his voice doesn't carry up to the second landing, so it might well be him. From the bedroom you can't hear the telly properly, but the smell of whisky is taking the place of turnips and there's a clattering of fists bumping on the table and shoes clacking on the floor, which mean it's probably HIGHLAND COUNTRY DANCING at the start of the show. Now someone's turned the telly up and I can just make out KENNETH MCKELLAR singing MY LOVE IS LIKE A RED RED ROSE before the CLUBBERS join in. Whoever was with Geo and Alec must have come up for the show because they're messing about happily again. If it's going to happen, it's got to happen in the next twenty-five minutes. Once he timed it just too late. That was great because you got all the excitement of waiting, and a result at the end, but none of the other stuff.

I put the book down, and lie back listening to the party going on down the hall. Mum's voice hovers unsteadily above the men's who won't get into their stride until a good fast number comes along and they can belt it out. Big Geo and Alec are replaying a decisive victory from last Saturday's league, Big Geo in all the star roles. They've forgotten all about me. I'm lying flat under the heavy blankets, looking up at the light, syrupy and orangey now that daylight has given up the fight.

They're laughing in the kitchen. ANDY STEWART. Or maybe they've got LEX McLEAN making a guest appearance, cause they're laughing quite loud. A door opens and I hold my breath, then the toilet flushes so I breathe out again, but I'm caught on the hop because it's him, he's come via the loo and now that I think about it there wasn't enough time between the door opening and the bog flushing to do any-thing. He smiles and so do I and there's all the usual stuff about how're you doing and feeling any better and I haven't heard you practising tonight. He sits on the bed and says how it's a shame, being stuck in here all on my own and no-one ever bothers to come in and see me. He's right, and he knows I'm pleased that at least someone has. He slaps the blankets where my legs are and asks if I'm not awful hot in there. My leg is where he's left his hand. Then he pulls the blankets up and waves them in front of my face, to fan me.

They've stopped laughing in the kitchen. Mum's duetting with MOIRA ANDERSON for HE-RE HE-RO MY BONNIE WEE LASS while he loosens up his trousers and jiggles, which looks quite funny, until his nob stands up like THE CAT-IN-THE-HAT'S hat, too tall to be real and bent at the end like it's been bashed. Then comes the bit I hate most, apart from the very last bit. His hand in my jammies stumbles around from my belly button to my legs and finally gets a hold of me and wiggles me, which is tickly and I have to try very hard so as not to burst out laughing. He hates it when I laugh. He closes his eyes and throws his head back like he's listening very carefully to Mum and MOIRA ANDERSON's song. The roar from the crowd provided by Alec for Big Geo's decisive goal makes him turn to the window and half open his eyes. Then he shuts them tighter and pulls my hand over.

I've always got to use two hands, which makes me think now that maybe the visits predate SMUGGLERS TOP. Maybe it was the SECRET SEVEN period. His nob's too big for one hand to go all the way round. I have to hang on with both hands and pull back and forwards like he told me to. Up and down up and down, up and down to the tune of THERE WAS A SOLDIER, A SCOTTISH SOLDIER. The pumping gets easier as you go along, once he starts to go all wet and soapy. But after a while my wrists get sore. I tried to tell him that one time, but he went berserk and said he'd tell Mum he'd just come up to say hello and found me playing with myself. He said that was what happened, first time. I can't remember that, but I'll give him the benefit of the doubt. Anyway, all I wanted was a rest for a minute, but I learned that that's not on. I can't hear ANDY STEWART now for the CLUBBERS all thrashing out THOSE GREEN HILLS ARE NOT HIGHLAND HILLS and I swear the visitor is mouthing the words as he bumps around. I wonder if I should sing, too. Towards the end you have to remember to turn your face away before the splashy bit, which most of the time ends up on my pillow and I have to tell Mum I spilt the hot milk at suppertime. They get to the last chorus in the kitchen. THOSE ARE NOT THE HILLS OF . . .

HOME! and everyone claps and yells and he puts everything back where it was.

At every visit I hope he's not going to do the last bit. The rest I can live with, but not that. Tonight he goes to the window and looks out. Geo and Alec are still out there, but I can't hear what they're playing at now. Then he comes back and I know he is going to do it. He never forgets. He kneels down beside my bed, and tells me to close my eyes. Then he bends his head forward over his joined hands. DEAR GOD, FORGIVE YOUR CHILDREN THEIR TRESPASSES and his eyes begin to water. He goes on and on until the hammering and clattering for the SCOTTISH COUNTRY DANCERS start up again at the end of the Show. As soon as the noise dies down he gets up quickly and goes to the door and he tells me that if I pray VERY VERY hard the GOOD GOD in all his MERCY will forgive me. That's the only time I want to cry. He smiles at me and tells me to take care now then he shuts the door and the visit's over.

In the kitchen the CLUBBERS are talking and laughing and the smell of whisky is strong and sweet. I get up out of bed and go to the window. It's pitch black outside. Big Geo and Alec are disappearing up the close. I wave but they don't see me. I wipe my hands on the curtain. The light and the fire have turned the room a mustard colour. It's like an oven in here after the fire's been on all day. But I'm still shivering. I take two spoonfuls of Ephedrine and hold the sticky syrup in my mouth. I hear the kitchen door open and jump into bed quick in case it's Mum with my supper and she gives me a row for getting up.

Guilty Party

The room became a huge version of the Van der Graaf generator Mr Wilkie had shown us in Physics, the excitement flashing from body to body. This was a kill; a certain kill. All the better for there being no general sense of ill-ease – only one boy was guilty. The rest revelled in the sport, the blood-lust. The innocent exchanged glances and muted laughter with the cruel and the strong: who was it? Who amongst them had transformed Monday morning into a public execution? The poor bloody victim couldn't possibly give himself away now. Everyone knew his game plan: look and act as innocent and malevolent as the rest; attempt utter amazement when he was the one left standing – pathetically, hopelessly – alone.

Dundas did not take the sting out of the situation; did not seek to clear up the mystery unobtrusively, or behind closed doors. He lead the frenzy from the front, opting to conduct the proceedings in open court. Once he got us all standing, and the babble had died away to a breathless hiss, he began chanting out the names.

RAFFERTY Arse-licker. Expert one. Not too impeccably uniformed, not too clever. Breaks the odd minor rule calculated to make the school body politic embrace him more, not less. Decent footballer.

CALDER Boys' own fucking hero. Brains he uses on inferiors like chibs. Captaincy potential for the rugby team means he gets away with murder. Last year, orchestrated a brilliant attack on the 1st years' rugby bus: eight underlings threw half-bricks at the drivers' window, smashing it to smithereens. Two of the underlings caught, but no police action. Naturally, no-one shops Calder. Disappointed when not even one of the kids or the driver gets hospitalised when the bus thwacked into the annexe.

LEE Wee Lee. Struts around like he's a hard man; say hello to Wee Lee, and it's like you've called him a runt. So no-one talks to him; he's happy about that.

Was Dundas at it? He seemed to be going through the jotters in the order he was given them, passed down from the back, collected at the front from the left row through to the right. But those three names were out of sequence. And they were dead cert innocents. There were thirty in the class, but only twenty-nine jotters with punishment exercises and names on them. One virgin jotter. One boy whose last desperate hope was about to be blown. Dundas was enjoying this, the shite. Prolonging it. Giving his troops a treat. He knew who it was. Everybody knew who it was.

NOBLE Frankie punched the air. Not him. There was a moment, though. Could have been him. Smelly wee guy, waster. Disorganised. Can be nasty in a crowd. Would be caught out later in 5th year. Some poor wino in the model house down the road standing on a top-storey ledge, drunk, threatening suicide. Daft bastard, does it during the school dinner time. A bunch of our uniforms are down below yelling up at him: 'Jump ya cunt! Jump ya cunt!' The wino does. Cops it. Arms and legs twisted around him like he'd sicked them up. Frankie's the only one huckled by the police. Frankie likes the pack; hates being picked out.

SOBOLEWSKI Nah. Marius knows to keep his head down. Avoid eye contact whenever possible. Do everything you're told by everyone. Do it just enough, in case you alienate another group. Go through it all again. Anyway, he's good at maths.

MACFARLANE Day one at school and McFarlane's the type anyone with any nous knows to avoid like the plague. Spick and span. Grafter. Even pisses off the powers-that-be who think he's bright but boring. MacFanny never broke a rule in his life.

EDWARDS Wasn't him. Who cares.

CONNELL Willie Connell looks around the room, smiling – if you can call it that: Willie Connell's smile is merely the accumulation of even more saliva than normal around his thin, pink little lips, like worms. Connell divides opinion equally. Those who fear him, and those who are either in with him or in with other vicious bastards up the school who are up to him. This person is pure evil. Nearly as small as Wee Lee, stupider even than Martin Edwards, but this class, this year, is his. It's his unfailing instinct to sniff out disharmony and turn it to violent chaos that does it. This is how he wins the respect of the Calders, Chalmers and Murrays of this world. And the Dundas's. Early on in 1st year, Connell selected his chief victim, Mickey Armstrong, probably at random, from amongst the boys that were already shiting themselves. He marks the poor bastard out for life. He comes in one day, with something secret, something menacing, in a plastic bag. He waits till afternoon break, then reveals it to his disciples: a used sanitary towel of his sister's. He orders Armstrong's seizure, and ties it on Armstrong like a necklace, with the laces of his football boots. At the end of the break he douses it in lighter fuel and torches it, Armstrong screaming like fuck.

Thing that struck me – there's a Connell *sister*? What's *she* like for Chrissakes?

For the rest of his school life Mickey Armstrong's known universally as The Pad.

Faint deflation of disappointment at Connell's name being called so early in the proceedings. Dundas himself read it out mournfully. Had Connell been the miscreant, the kick would have been all the greater. Not only the delight in his capture, but the exhilarating possibility that Willie Connell might well retaliate. The boy's reaction to any given situation was always exceptional; to an unpleasant situation, always alarming. Dundas would have liked the challenge. A man like Dundas needs new material to sustain his infamy.

Still, good that the hunt hadn't finished so soon. This was a roller-coaster, gathering thrill as it picked up speed. From such a minor initial transgression, who'd have guessed the culprit's strategy would have had such an effect. Dundas went back to the pile of jotters: there were other juicy possibilities ahead.

DEWER: He sat down before his name was called, knowing his jotter was under Willie Connell's. A dunce. Often in trouble, half the time on his mentor's behalf. Dewer is the worm-lipped little shit's aide accomplice. The passer of information, the spreader of rumours, the fall guy, when one is needed.

Dundas paused for a moment, considered castigating Dewer for seating himself before the evidence of his innocence was made public. But, a good tactician, he knew to avoid the deflection. His boys were in thrall. Don't divert them from the central plot: the pursuit and inevitable capture of a boy so stupid, or so frightened, of failing to return a punishment exercise that he has sent the entire class on this blood-thirsty man-hunt.

DAVIDSON
STEWART
HUGHES
MCBRIDE

Names of boys who had the fortune not to stand out, not to provoke any reaction, either good or bad. Survivors, with the ability to lose ourselves in the general classness. A lesson we all learnt for life.

HODGE There are those who believe so utterly in their own abilities that everyone around them ends up believing in them too. And this without a scrap of extrinsic evidence.

WALLS Wallsy. Hodge gone wrong. Brighter, but without the winning smile and the silver tongue that everyone believes Hodge to possess. Hodge is the smart-arse you had to pretend to like, Wallsy's the smart-arse you can safely ignore.

REECE Star-crossed. In later life he would play professional football, sign a recording deal, qualify from Cambridge with honours, spawn several photo-copies of himself and his model wife, all of them talented, rich and polished. At this point in his career, he gets 90% for everything, captains the third year football, fencing and debating teams, is followed around by girls from the co-ed across the road, and never, ever, gets into the shit. Bastard of it is, he's okay.

CHALMERS Andy's the only guy no-one wants to be guilty. Crazy Andy. Crap footballer but keen. Hails from the same scheme as Willie Connell. Usually in trouble with the authorities, but seldom serious stuff. Matey with everyone; completely ignores (or is unaware of) the class frontiers –

tribal lines no-one but Andy can cross. Mates with Connell, but still advises The Pad on how to deal with him. The advice isn't worth the soiled towel that is Paddy's scholastic birthright, but at least he makes the effort. No-one else does. Teachers think him thick as shit. Maybe he is; lucky man.

The numbers have dwindled to a handful. Five kids left standing, all covered in studied innocence, sheer astonishment at not being off the hook yet. Dundas sniffs the mood of the class: getting impatient. We want a result. There's no question now, anyway. Dundas knows that. Knows that we know that. We want our prey quickly. Cut to the chase.

HALLIDAY

MCSWEEN

Barked out in quick succession. A pair of uniforms, indistinguishable from one another, sit down. There's no air left in the classroom now. We've sucked it all into our lungs and it's not coming back out again. Dundas is a mean bitch at the best of times, but after this?

GALT Traitor.

JORDAN Stereotype heavy. Big jaws, big hair, big, black jacket. In third year he gets riled at the jokes about the size and hirsuteness of his male member. By 5th year he'll be pulling it out at every available opportunity, especially when the tarts from across the way congregate at the gate to coo at Jonathon Reece. No-one has an opinion on Jordan. It'd be like discussing the personality of a urinal.

At last, the guilty boy is left standing alone; it's the only time he towers above his seated persecutors. He's swaying, nearly fainting, the practised expression of surprise, who me? not sticking to his terrified face. Dundas pauses for a very, very long time. Then softly, almost gently, whispers his name.

ARMSTRONG.

The Pad's last friend had deserted him. Bernie Galt always

copied The Pad's homework and punishment exercises. The price Armstrong had to pay for the only flicker of friendship in this life. This morning Galt says, sorry. He says he remembered his own jotter, but forgot Mickey Armstrong's. The Pad, though, like everyone else in the class (Dundas included probably) saw him slip it to Willie Connell. So the Pad pulled a new jotter out of his bag, hands it in, hopes to fuck that it won't be noticed till after break. The Pad's not bad at maths, he could do the exercise again during French, hand it in to Dundas, all apologies. He made two mistakes: 1) should have put his name on it; and 2) knows fine well Dundas can smell blood before he gets out his bed in the morning.

Connell's face goes limp and sated, licks the excess saliva from his chin. Mickey Armstrong's face has the same expression it's had for three years now: total defeat, total terror. The room goes quiet; the pack showing disciplined restraint. They look to their leader: Dundas casts his eye about the room. Give the boys what they want. He turns to The Pad. Sneers. Crooks his finger.

'Paddy.' He says.

The Milch Cow

Christine Shaw was hiding at the back of the barn when she saw Caitlin Campbell drink milk directly from the cow's udder. She saw her kneel down beside one of the cows, take the teat between her fingers, knead it gently till the milk began to flow, then bow her head and drink. From the shadows at the back of the barn, Christine watched her stand up, saw her lips and neck coated with warm white milk, which misted lightly in the cold morning air and rose around her face and hair like a halo.

Then Caitlin wiped her mouth on her sleeve, tiptoed back to the door, and left, shutting the door tight behind her. Christine followed her out, and watched her head down through the fields. From up here, the town looked as if it had been snapped off from the city and left to rot in the grey fields. The Glasgow ring road links up a whole string of towns like this – broken beads on a cheap necklace. Caitlin emerged from the fields at the bottom of the hill and climbed up on the motorway, walking west towards the city. No-one ever saw Caitlin Campbell again.

Soon after, Christine Shaw graduated from the Job Search Programme and replaced Caitlin as Milk Maid on the Gadaiche Dubh Estate. There, she also replaced Caitlin in the attentions of Robert Urquhart, heir to the Estate. A boon for a townie like her, Robert being the only local lad able to offer a comfortable home and hearth to some lucky girl. Eventually, they made love one night in the barn, just as Christine had watched him and Caitlin do before. Caitlin called Robert 'her stallion', and though Christine had nothing to compare him against, she thought he took her like a young Chevalier.

– Are you on the pill, Christine? He asked when they were done.

She shook her head.

– Then better safe than sorry. Grandfather assures me the best precaution is milk, straight from the udder, the morning after. The old ways are often the best.

– Does it work?

– It has for me in the past.

She waited till he had gone, then picked up a stool and went into one of the byres. She sat down and massaged the teat, the way Robert had trained her, until the creamy white milk began to flow. She lowered her head and, brushing her hair aside, tasted a drop on her tongue. It tasted hot and pungent. She took another drop, and another, then washed her face with the milk on her hands.

Christine Shaw left the barn and walked through the frozen fields, looking over towards town, as the morning mist congealed. On the motorway, she headed towards Glasgow, the cars spitting by her and sounding their horns, and the milk turning sweet in her mouth.

Spring

When the boys came down for breakfast she was already there, sitting up at a table at the back. They went about the business of piling eggs and fried bread and tomatoes on their plates, nudging each other and glancing over at her. Brown Jumper joined in with the nudging, but half-heartedly, providing the minimum necessary to avoid suspicion. He walked to a table with Yellow Jersey and tried to beat him to the seat facing away from her.

– No, no, Yellow Jersey said. – Be my guest. Feast your eyes.

She was talking to a girl who had her back to the boys. White T-shirt ambled up to the window behind the women, supposedly checking the weather, and came back to report.

– Other one must be the old one's daughter. Gorgeous, by the way. Jail-bait, but not worth a ten-year stretch.

– Age before beauty, I'll settle for the old dear, Yellow jersey said, and Brown Jumper laughed dutifully with the rest, then tried to concentrate on his breakfast.

But every time he looked up, he timed it just wrong. She was always looking over in his direction, smiling. He tried to smile back once without the boys noticing, but his facial muscles refused to tighten on him and the best he could do was nod limply. The boys clocked that and slagged him for being Joe Cool. It pissed him off, but he tried not to show it. Show it, and they'll never stop.

She must have just showered before she came down, because her hair was still damp. She popped nibbles of food with freshly-scrubbed hands into her bright mouth, and her lemony skin rippled round her eyes when she smiled. Like a warm morning she made him feel comfortable and calm. But when she got up to help herself to more coffee, the motion of her body breezing soap smells as she passed their table, he imagined the smell of her, naked: coriander and bay. Brown Jumper was no better than the rest of them. He got up and left.

That was a mistake. The boys sensed his agitation and for the rest of the morning Brown Jumper's unspoken hots for the woman were the topic of the day. He was just getting moody about it when, sensing it, the boys changed the focus from the woman to the girl.

– A sweetie she was. Trouble is – White T-shirt said – I can't decide if I want to hump her or adopt her.

Brown Jumper acquitted himself admirably:

– If you were that Woody Allen, maybe you could do both.

That got a laugh and after that they laid off him about the woman.

But at night they were all having a few beers standing at the hotel bar, when the woman comes in again. Brown

Jumper's heart sank. She was alone this time. White T-Shirt wondered if she had left Jail Bait's room unlocked. She said good evening, enough in Brown Jumper's direction for a couple of the boys to elbow him in the stomach and raise an eyebrow. She sat behind them, so he turned away from her and faced the bar. He could feel her behind him, hear the rustle of her clothes as she moved. She was the centre of gravity in the room which seemed to capsize in her direction behind him. And when he had to turn around a little when conversation was directed to him, he caught sight of her out of the corner of his eye, reading her paper. She was more convivial sitting alone, than he was surrounded by his mates. The morning smile still lingered somewhere around her lips. Her eyes swept over the page of the paper in front of her, then up into the room, and he managed to turn away before her gaze landed on him. Looking through the gantry he saw her lying naked next to him, absorbing his body into hers. He kept the image for a moment, then let it go, re-tuned into the boys standing around him, and wished that he were alone. Away from the boys and, especially, away from the woman, who made him feel so heavy and torpid and stupid.

The waiter said their table was ready now if they'd like to move through. Brown Jumper mapped out the move first in his mind, then turned the long way round from the bar so he wouldn't have to face her. Automatically, he pulled his shoulders back and his belly in, though really he didn't want her to look at him at all. Getting his jacket from the back of his chair and grabbing his pint from the bar top involved a complicated series of movements. He didn't manage it. The jacket fell first, then the glass dropped on to it, soaking it with beer.

First there was the laughter of the boys. But then, through it, her laughter, like the first drops of rain after thunder. It was a soft, unaccusing sound that made him want to turn round and share in it too. A little accident of life that connects strangers. He felt the boys behind him turn to her and laugh with her. He wanted to do the same. He wanted to turn and let her eyes shower him in their cool light. But he couldn't. He stood motionless for a moment, gripped by a freezing anger. He turned, and without seeing her, hissed:

– Who the fuck are you laughing at?

He couldn't believe he'd said it. Two of the boys came up at either side of him, and led him gently away, saying it's all right now, forget it. And he was glad they were there, because he knew that really, they understood.

Auntie Mary

Auntie Mary's dead, or so she claims. Been that way for years.

You go:

– Fancy a cup of tea, Mary?

And she smiles and rolls her eyes as if to say how could you be so stupid:

– Dead people don't drink tea, son.

She'll end up having the tea all right, but only after a decent argy-bargy. You have to have your wits about you, though. She's as sharp as a razor is Auntie Mary. What you *can't* do, is tackle the basic premise of her argument: the fact that she is dead. You *can* try something like:

– I don't know about that, Mary. Dead peoples' hair and fingernails grow, yes?

– You're not kidding. I spend half my life cutting my nails.

Don't think you're onto something here with the 'half my life' bit. We've all picked up on that. Mary just replies: figure of speech, son, figure of speech. No flies on Mary.

– Never had such good strong nails when I was alive.

– Well, then. For things to grow they need nourishment. Am I right? So drink your tea.

Or take your medicine, or eat your dinner, or whatever it is you're trying to get her to do. Put on some clothes. Have a drink at Christmas. Actually that one isn't so hard – for a dead person she fair likes her Martinis.

This approach isn't without its perils, however. Sometimes it can bring her round to her favourite argument.

– It's the earth that nourishes. So bury me.

Auntie Mary's not daft. Nor, in my opinion, is she particularly crazy. She's a bright wee thing. Usually pretty cheery, too. She's the youngest of my aunts and uncles, only about ten years older than me, and therefore much easier to relate to. The death thing doesn't come up all that often. And most of the time it can be got out the way quickly enough. Except when she gets on to being buried. And then it's like everyone's being unfair to her, not doing the decent thing and giving her what she wants.

– Dead people ought to be buried. It's a crying shame leaving me here like this.

I was only about eight or nine when they found her outside in the hospital grounds, clawing away at the earth, digging a big hole with her bare hands. She'd just been told that the baby she was carrying was dead. Uncle Marty – I can't remember him – couldn't handle it. Went ballistic by all accounts. Some big scene up in the ward that nobody talks about now.

Anyway, Mary's all right now. She does book-keeping at home for some accountant or other and spends most of the proceeds on sweets and toys for the kids. My lot love going there. Auntie Mary's the bees-knees. They don't mind her being dead, and it doesn't seem to get in the way of her talking or making cakes or playing with the kids. Just at birthdays and Christmas and the like, when Mary's had a wee Martini or two, you have to keep your eye on the back green.